Y0-BVG-026

MYSTERY HOUSE

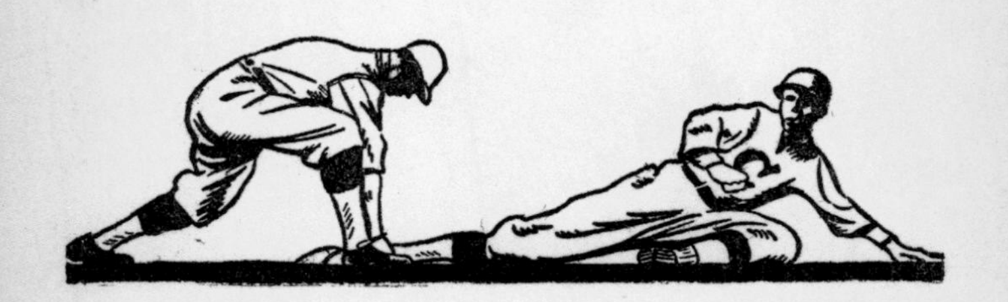

A cluster of men was out at the reef's end

MYSTERY HOUSE

BY

R. J. BURROUGH

ILLUSTRATED BY

LEE TOWNSEND

GROSSET & DUNLAP

PUBLISHERS NEW YORK

By Arrangement with Longmans, Green and Co.

BURROUGH
MYSTERY HOUSE

PRINTED IN THE UNITED STATES OF AMERICA

ILLUSTRATIONS

MYSTERY HOUSE

CHAPTER I

GLANCING at his wrist watch, Smiley Adams ran down the rain-soaked porch steps of his aunt's house in Black Hill, Maine.

"O. K." he called to the two in the driveway. "Meet me down at the Post Office. The sun's out to stay, at least for a little while."

"What?" Bill Warrener, lolling at ease at the wheel of his father's red roadster, snapped off the ignition and Dick Scarlett, trying to crank the car, straightened up, his face red and dripping with sweat.

"Meet me at the Post Office," Smiley repeated. "I'm going down to see if they've sent us any word from home. And get a move on if we're going to see the wreck before high tide."

"All right." Dick's head disappeared behind the nickel rim of the radiator, on which the sun beat warmly.

"Yeah," Bill amended, "if we get her cranked in time."

"We?" Smiley turned around with a quizzical look. "Seems to me Dick's doing all the work."

"Sure," Bill conceded amiably. "But I'm doing all the brain work. And that's what counts."

Dick's hot face shot into view. "Cut that out, Bill. I'm sick of your guff. No one, to listen to you, would think it's your fault the battery's near dead. You left her dry as a bone!"

Bill's tolerant laugh echoed in Smiley's ears as he started down the deserted, sunlit street. "Bill will get his some day," he thought. "It's coming to him."

He had to step over great branches torn from the trees during the storm of the last two days. The May sun, warm on his back, as he went along, was drying the carpet of rain-drenched leaves.

Smiley looked up at the sky, full of swift moving clouds. It still held hint of the gale which, howling in from the sea, had for the past two days lashed the little coast village; had shaken the small white houses. Rain had swept like a gray sheet across the country, beating down everything that reared a head from the soaked earth.

It was during this gale that the three-master, *Nellie Saunders,* beaten far off her course in the wild smother, had piled up on Destruction Reef, a needle-like ledge of rocks, stretching a quarter mile out to sea. The bottom had been ripped out of her as she struck full, her foghorn bellowing helplessly.

The boat from the lighthouse at Destruction Head, a mile down the coast, had put out to her and got all but one of her crew off before she sank. It was this wreck the boys were going down to see.

"Phew!" Smiley hopped across an uprooted tree. "It's getting hotter." He shoved his open windbreaker back on his shoulders.

On the other side of the street and a little before the Post Office was the high school, a big red brick building with gym and athletic field attached. Here men were setting up arc lights, evidently in preparation for the next night's baseball game. A group of boys in baseball uniform, blue sweaters slung over their arms, was straggling lackadaisically onto the diamond, a muddy, dark brown patch.

"Humph," Smiley commented, "not a very peppy looking bunch."

They certainly weren't as they moved sullenly across to the benches and, throwing down their sweaters, settled themselves there, squinting as the sun struck full in their eyes. They kept glancing uneasily back at the gym, exchanging muttered comments that Smiley couldn't catch as he passed on the other side of the narrow street.

Suddenly the door of the gym was flung open and a hulking youngster in uniform shot down the steps. At the foot he swung around, his ruddy face twisted with anger, and shook his fist at the closed door.

"Here's Cole!"

Shouting, the others sprang up and crowded around the newcomer, their arms slung across each other's shoulders, their heads nodding appreciatively at what he was telling them. Every now and then one of them let out a whoop of admiration and then shoved closer so as not to miss a word.

"What're they so hopped up about?" Smiley wondered. He had his hand on the knob of the Post Office door when, like magic, the group on the athletic field broke up, the players drifting apart, muttering. He couldn't hear what they were saying, but he soon saw the cause of the disbanding.

Down the gym steps had come a young man, the coach evidently, a white sweater over his street clothes.

The players crowded together belligerently and stared at him.

"All right," he snapped. "We've got to get in a little batting practise before noon. No real play or base running, of course; the ground's too muddy. But you've got to get your batting eyes sharpened up if you're to make any kind of showing tomorrow night. You, Treworgy, get out there and warm up. You catch him, Cole. The rest of you take your bats and get out on the line."

His orders moved the glum-looking squad around.

Smiley frowned, puzzled, as he went into the cool Post Office. The face of that coach was familiar. He knew he had seen it somewhere. The fellow was only a little older than Smiley, a couple of years or so. He seemed to be about twenty and he certainly had his hands full with that team. Where had he seen him before?

Smiley was half way across the floor when he remembered, and stopped dead in surprise. "Whew!" he whistled. "Craig, I'll bet a stamp! Say, Mr. McIntyre!" Smiley rapped on the General Delivery window and stuck his head inside. "Who's that coach for the baseball team?"

Pop McIntyre, Postmaster of the Black Hills Station, swung around from his high desk, shoving back his eyeshade. "Why, hello, Smiley. What? Why, that's Jim Craig, the young feller from Dartmouth."

"That's what I thought," Smiley nodded. "The soph pitcher who beat every team he met and had all the big league scouts trying to sign him up?"

"That's right." Pop beamed as if every word were true of himself. "Then he comes down here.

Give 'em all the slip. Didn't go back to college this year. Nobuddy knows why, but they say — mind you," Pop lowered his eyebrows in a warning frown, "I'm not sure, but they say there's something queer about him. He hired that old house 'bout ten mile down th' coast — "

"Live all alone?" Smiley stemmed the tide for a minute.

"Doan't know. Nobuddy knows. Foalks call the place 'Mystery House.' He's got a dog big as a bull, Lem Tuttle says, minds it night an' day and nobuddy's been inside. He doan't talk none, 'ceptin' to the team, and not much to them since he had a run-in with Cole, their best player. Foalks thinks it mighty funny. He's got a boat and — by the way," Pop broke himself off, "have you been to see the wreck, down to Destruction Reef?"

"No." Smiley shook his head. "But we're going down there right now, though, if we — "

"Well," Mr. McIntyre was off again, "he saved those men from the *Nellie Saunders,* Jim Craig did. Yep." He nodded his head. "He lives down there by the coast, 'bout ten miles. You'll pass it on your way, only house beside Lem Tuttle's out that way. Well, he heard the foghorn bellerin' through all the blow. He beat it down to the shore; couldn't take his boat himself, waves was too mighty high, so he legged it to the lighthouse. They'd 'a' been goners if it hadn't been fer Jim, though I declare I doan't know how he made it. Rain was so thick you couldn't see your hand afore you. I hed to go out to m' shed 'bout five o'clock to milk Bessie." Pop bit himself a chew of tobacco and hunched down over the counter. "I went out to milk Bessie and I hed to tell Mother to stand there in th' door with a lamp or I'd clean lost my way. Even as 'twas I hed a time, and 'twarn't more than thutty feet. That blow's not over yet nuther."

"Well, we're going down right away," Smiley broke in. "Is there any mail for us?"

Pop's face, all set to smile, frowned instead. "Is that big boy with the little red car visitin' down to your aunt's with you?"

"Yes." Smiley nodded, scanning the old man's face and hoping against hope that Bill hadn't been up to some more of his show-off tricks. "Why?"

"Nothin'," the other said slowly, "only I hear that Ollie Masters down to the drug store's got it in fer 'im. Seems the boy went in there three nights ago, afore the storm, and wanted something Ollie hadn't in stock, so he got mighty sassy. Called Ollie a dum' old hick and a lot of other stuff."

"I'm sorry," Smiley said. "That's too bad. Well, any mail for us, Mr. McIntyre?"

The postmaster jerked open a drawer. "Eeyeah. I think ther's one." He adjusted his spectacles and shuffled rapidly through a slim pile. "Yes, here 'tis."

"Thanks." Smiley slit the envelope open. "Now let's hope it's not what I think it is."

He read rapidly through the first page of his mother's letter and grinned. "Great! We don't have to go back yet."

He glanced up at Mr. McIntyre who was squinting interestedly at the note. "Our high school had a fire last week and they gave us this time off so they could get the place in shape. But mother says nothing's finished and classes don't begin Monday. Well, so long. I have to break the news to Dick and Bill."

Once out in the street Smiley frowned. The word about going home wasn't all that had been in the letter. He had skipped the part where his mother said, "What's this I hear about Bill? His father's very angry about some word he received that his car plowed through a herd of cows on your way down!"

Smiley stood there reading this part again, cogitating his mother's reaction. He shook his head and creasing the letter absentmindedly stuck it in his pocket. Bill had it coming to him and the day couldn't be far away. He had too good an opinion of himself and now it was getting him into trouble. Time and time again Bill himself said, admiringly and wonderingly, "Boy, I'm good. I'm so good I don't realize it myself. I don't know yet just how good I am. I've never even been extended."

And the funny part of it was that Bill was right. He *was* good. Star football man, he put every ounce of his brawn into playing fullback. A great baseball player, noted for his terrific slugging. Anchor man on the swimming team. On down the line there was only one thing Bill couldn't do, and that he had never even dreamed of trying; to be modest about himself and his accomplishments.

Smiley and Dick, his two best friends, had been at him constantly till they had to give up in despair, realizing that Bill really did have good qualities which others who knew only his blustery, loud-mouthed way never suspected. For one thing he was absolutely loyal. He'd fight at the drop of the hat and against any odds to help a friend.

On the trip down to Smiley's aunt's, Bill had been pretty hard to get along with, with his loud and long denunciations of the "stupid dumbbells of hicks" when the road was blocked, as it often was, by sheep and rumbling ox-carts.

"Well," Smiley thought, starting back slowly along the sunny street, "if we can keep him reasonably quiet until we get him home, all right."

He glanced idly ahead down the street where practise was still going on, then, at what he saw, sprinted ahead.

Trouble! And plenty of it.

There, parked beside the playing field, was the familiar red roadster. There was Bill, lounging back of the batter's cage, commenting on plays and players. Dick, angry-looking, was trying to get him away.

As Smiley came up he took in the situation at a glance. The young coach, dissatisfied with the way one of the squad was batting, had grabbed the man's bat and was himself giving a lesson in stance and swing.

"All right, Treworgy," he called to the pitcher, his voice clear and incisive but with an irritated edge to it. Evidently Bill's remarks had got under the skin.

The pitcher growled something to his mates, then doubled himself into a knot and shot a fast one straight for the coach's head.

Craig leaped back, holding his bat high to avoid being hit.

"Sorry," the pitcher mumbled. Then he shot a sidelong grin at Bill.

The coach didn't say a word as he stepped back into the box and tapped his bat against the plate.

Cole, the catcher, tossed the ball back to the mound, with an undisguised laugh.

Again Treworgy shot it for the plate.

This time Craig tipped it, and the ball popped a

few feet into the air. The catcher, slinging off his mask, camped under it, and caught it, an easy pop fly.

The players snickered.

"Hurray!" Bill boomed, pounding on the wire netting of the cage. "Hurray for nothing!"

Slowly the coach turned around, his face reddening. Then, dropping the bat to the ground, he walked across to Bill who waited there calmly, giving him eye for eye.

"Listen, kid," Craig began. "We don't want you hanging around here blatting about something you don't know the first thing about. Get going!"

"Oh, I don't think so," Bill responded easily, rocking slowly back and forth on his heels. "I like it here. It's better than a circus and lots cheaper. Besides I'll tell you when you teach them wrong."

The coach stepped closer. "Get this," he said, his eyes narrowing. "Either shut up or put up. You think you can get out there and hit?"

"Come on, Bill," Smiley broke in. "Don't be a chump. This coach is a pitcher, not a batter."

"Same thing." Bill was expansive. "I bet he's no better as a pitcher."

"Want to try it?" the young fellow asked quietly, keeping his temper down with an effort; he must have been conscious of the snickering going on behind his back.

"Sure." Bill stepped onto the diamond with a laugh. "I'll show you how."

"Say, Smiley," Dick protested, "we can't let him carry on like this. He's crazy."

"Wait a minute." Smiley held Dick back, and a grin cut across his face. "He'll get his all right. D'you know who that coach is? Craig, of Dartmouth. The soph pitcher who won every game last season and broke the strike-out record. If he could fool those college batters, what'll he do to a high school kid? Let Bill go out there. He's got it coming!"

"Craig?" Dick repeated uncertainly. Then remembrance began to dawn. "Boy," he spluttered gleefully, "Bill gets his right here!"

Out on the diamond the players were clustered around the plate, silent, yet ready to break out any minute.

The young coach picked up a fielder's mitt, thumped his clenched fist into it venomously and walked out to the rubber. He tossed in a few practise pitches, the ball coming in nicely for perfect strikes, after he got the range.

Bill watched disdainfully, not even troubling to remove his windbreaker.

"Ready?" Craig snapped.

Bill gave a mocking salute and stepped up to the plate, taking an easy stand and swinging the bat nonchalantly, one hand on his hip. This bit of grandstand play wasn't missed by the team. He said something to the catcher, Cole, about "hick pitcher" and Smiley saw the coach's lips tighten grimly.

"Oh," Smiley snorted in disgust, "look at him. The old show-off. He'll get his all right." He breathed it as if it were a prayer.

Craig wound up.

"The pitch," Dick cried unnecessarily.

Thud! The ball was in the catcher's mitt before Bill could even offer at it, a perfect strike.

The backstop straightened up, tossed the ball back to the mound in silence.

Now Bill was watching more closely. He was gripping the bat with both hands, swinging it slowly, watching the pitcher with an eagle eye.

Again Craig wound up.

Bill crouched tensely, bat at the height of his shoulder.

The pitch came in.

STR-R-IKE TWO!

Bill had tied himself into a knot swinging at a slow ball. Smiley thought it the slowest he had ever seen. He could almost count the stitches on it as it came sailing up, looking as big as a balloon.

Bill shifted his footing and took a toehold.

Smiley and Dick nudged each other delightedly, and Craig permitted his expression to relax as he rubbed the ball a bit in his hands. He glanced at his squad, a sullen-looking lot, watching every move.

Slowly he took his next wind-up and shot the ball for the plate.

CRACK!

Bill, putting all the strength of his tremendous shoulders into a vicious swing had reached out for the pitch, a bad ball, had caught it square on the nose and it had started back. It was still rising as it sailed by the gaping electricians and over the top of the stands.

The players howled and clapped, Cole the loudest of all, but there was no good feeling about them. They were frankly glad that their coach had lost.

Smiley frowned as Bill, a cocky grin on his lips, sauntered toward him and Dick. He swung along casually with never a look behind him at the shouting, applauding team.

The coach came after Bill. "Wait a minute," he called.

Bill swung around, his grin deepening.

"That was a mighty sweet hit," Craig began.

But Bill held up his hand. "That was easy," he said modestly, and made for the roadster. "Come around some time and I'll show you how to do it," he flung over his retreating shoulder.

Craig looked at Smiley and Dick as if he couldn't believe his ears.

"I'm mighty sorry this happened," Smiley said apologetically.

"That's all right," Craig brushed aside his apology. "Only keep your friend away. One of these hicks he despises so much might take a swing at him. Meaning me!"

Bill was honking the horn impatiently. "C'mon, you two," he yelled.

"It can't be long now, Smiley," Dick growled. "If I have to do it myself!"

Smiley nodded. "And I'll be there," he promised. Behind him he heard Craig dismissing the squad and the roar which followed.

"Why did he do that?" he thought. "Now they'll think they've got him on the run. He should have worked them till they dropped in their tracks."

"Well," Bill began, as he slid into first and the wheels spun a bit on the wet, grassy edge of the road, "I guess I showed that dumbhead up all right, didn't I?"

Smiley yawned loud and long, insultingly, and stretched himself with a series of grunts.

A loose link in the tire chain banged against the fender.

"Say!" Bill demanded angrily as he turned out of the deserted main street and into a narrow country road. "What's the idea of giving me th' bird?"

Smiley jerked his feet down from the instrument

panel and planked them on the floor deliberately. "Listen, Bill," he looked at the other boy coldly, "you're about the most gosh-awful chump that ever was. You're good, yes, but no one in the world can get away with the stuff you pull. It was bad enough when it hurt no one but yourself, but today you went the limit."

"What're you jawing about?" Bill growled.

"Just this. That fellow Craig was having a hard enough time with that bunch of rubes before you butted in, but your smart-aleck stunt will make it just that much harder for him. Do you know who he is? Craig of Dartmouth."

Bill was staggered for a second. "Craig? What's he doing—" But then he stopped. "Just goes to show how good I am," he decided.

"You never quit playing the whale, do you, Bill?" Dick put in admiringly.

"What you mean?" Bill looked at him suspiciously.

"Thar she blows!"

"Well," Bill came back slowly, "don't you kiddies worry about it. 'S no importance."

Smiley gritted his teeth.

The ride developed into an endurance contest in silence as they sped, clanking, along the narrow lane.

Presently it branched to the right where a weather-beaten signboard pointed the way to Destruction Light, but they continued straight ahead, passing a little clearing with a small, tumble-down farmhouse. The path to it was a faint line in the glistening grass. A gnarled apple tree in bloom, grew beside the door, wet velvet-black by the rain. Weeds straggled over a tip-tilted, rotting well-cover. The breeze bore the scent of lilacs from a great blowing clump at the edge of the road.

The banging of their chain travelled through the silent forest. As the lane paralleled the sea for a minute they caught glimpses of the water sparkling far below them, blue, deserted.

The first sign of human beings came about nine or ten miles from the village. Here was a farm, the Tuttle place, Smiley imagined, the usual huddle of barns and house joined together for protection against the winter. A creaking wagon loaded with lumber was just pulling into the farmyard. The driver halted his sweating horses. They all turned and looked at the red roadster scooting along the muddy lane.

"Take it easy, Bill," Dick shouted as they jolted over a rock. "You'll bust her springs."

Bill grunted and kept up his speed. A startled rabbit which had been sitting in the middle of the way scuttled into the woods. The car swung wildly around a turn and the rear wheel scraped a rock. Before them was a large sign, planted in front of the trees, KEEP OUT. VICIOUS DOG.

A furious baying rang through the woods.

"This must be Craig's place, Dick, the place they call 'Mystery House.'"

Then they saw the house. It was set well back from the road in a broad clearing, a dark farmhouse, weather-beaten and with closely curtained windows. A huge, silver-fawn mastiff lunged with full-throated roars, the length of his chain, tangling himself around the great trunks of the trees in front of the house.

"Looks like the Hound of the Baskervilles," Dick cried as they sped past.

It was growing cooler and the unmistakable salt breath of the sea swept up to them.

"Here's where we've got to walk," Smiley said a few minutes later.

The lane had petered out in great sand dunes and only a faint wagon track led down to the shore.

Smiley saw that Bill was hesitating. "Don't go down there with the bus, Bill," he warned. "She won't be able to make it. That path's full of rocks and dips. She may get stuck in the sand. She can't make it!"

"Yes, she can," Bill contradicted confidently.

Smiley sucked in his breath and shook his head. He hopped out of the roadster. Dick followed and the two of them started down the bumpy track. Below them was the shore, the tide far past the turn, booming in. Smooth rollers, the kickup from the gale, foamed onto the beach. Gulls, whose tracks feather-stitched the sand, circled far out, screaming harshly.

"There's Destruction Reef!" Smiley pointed to a narrow ledge of jagged rocks stretching a good quarter-mile out. The edges of the reef were foam.

"Where'd the ship go down?" Dick questioned, searching the water for any signs of her.

"They didn't know in the village." Smiley's voice was loud enough to be heard above the waves as they neared the shore. "She might have gone down almost anywhere along here. It's eighty feet deep out at the tip and those are only the very tops of the rocks you see. They're covered by about a foot at high tide and they stretch way out under water."

"Sort of like a berg; most of it under."

Smiley nodded.

"Well, let's get out there and see if we can find her."

"No." Smiley shook his head. It's too dangerous. Folks around here avoid this reef. You're liable to slip on that seaweed and slide off into no telling what. We'll get a skiff from Mason down at the Light. He's still in Black Hill Hospital with his two sons but his wife's there and she'll let me have it."

They kept climbing steadily down. They were almost on the beach when they heard a terrific bumping and rattling behind them and swung around.

There was the roadster jerking her way toward them, jolting across rocks, dipping into gullies and grinding over rough ledges. Bill, with a yell, began to pound the horn, then stepped full on the gas and shot for the boys. They leaped into a mass of thorny bushes as Bill plunged past and out onto the damp but hard packed sand.

"The fool!" Smiley roared, scrambling back into the path. "I'll break every bone in his body!"

Bill swept across the great band of seaweed and driftwood which had been tossed up during the storm and snapped off his motor.

"Say," he cried, hopping out and pointing toward the end of the reef, "look at the mast!"

"Where?" Dick questioned. "I don't see any."

"Way out there—about two feet of her sticking up. C'mon out! I bet we can see her swell."

Smiley thought fiercely, "Let him go. He'll soon get a lesson and a good ducking too." But then he remembered the fear with which the natives regarded this place. "Don't go out there," he shouted, the words almost dragged out of him. "It's too dangerous. There are great cracks in those rocks you can't see under the weed. If you get caught or break a leg who's going to care about getting you out?"

"Ha, ha!" Bill derided, not even momentarily halted. "So the little boy's sore, huh? *And* afraid. Well, I'm going out, anyhow. If I get stuck my brains'll get me out. You coming, Dick?"

"No." Dick shook his head. "And you'd better not go either. You're a fool if you do."

Without answering, Bill started out along the pathway of uneven, seaweed-covered rocks, now only about four feet wide and only a few feet above the surface.

Dick and Smiley watched his figure getting smaller, watched the waves licking up at him until, when he looked about a half-inch high, he had reached the place where the ship had evidently gone down. They saw him bending over, peering into the deep water.

"Well, he made it," Dick commented glumly. "I never saw the beat. If we'd tried that we'd be flat on our faces in a minute. Look at him now!"

Bill had started back and, as though conscious that they were watching him, had begun to show off. He was leaping from one low hump of rock to another. He had his right arm clutched to his chest as though he were cuddling an imaginary football and his left was thrust out, straightarming an opponent. Now he shifted the ball to the other arm, and changed his pace as if dodging a would-be tackler. Then he leaped high out of the clutch of phantom fingers.

Dick grinned unwillingly. "Big show-off," he grunted. "Well, let's go get the boat." He started ahead.

"Wait a minute." Smiley was worried. "He may kill himself yet."

"Look here." Dick pointed to a fish evidently stranded during the storm. "What's this thing?"

Smiley shifted his gaze from the racing figure. "Oh, that's what the natives call a devil fish. They shoot out clouds of ink when they're attacked. There are crowds of them around here."

"I thought they all had tentacles. This one—"

"Dick!" Smiley cried. "Where is Bill? He was about half way in. Where is he?"

Their startled eyes searched the bare stretch of sparkling water, with only a narrow ledge of foam-licked rocks above the rolling surface.

There was no sign of Bill.

There was no sound above the boom of the surf and the plaintive cries of gulls.

CHAPTER II

The surf-beaten shore stretched deserted. On the shimmering sea Smiley could make out no swimming or floating object. Fishing gulls were the only moving things, swooping down, striking with a splash, then rising up on beating wings.

Straight ahead of the boys lay Destruction Reef with its treacherous, spray-dashed rocks. There was no sign of Bill here, either, but it was their only chance.

"Come on, Dick!" Smiley sped across the thick band of debris from the gale. Sea urchins' shells crunched under his running feet.

"Listen, Smiley," Dick shouted, his voice loud to carry above the waves. "It's another of his fool tricks. He'll get us out there like a couple of goats, then roar himself sick laughing at us." But Dick followed his chum.

"There's no place for him to hide unless he gets down in the water," Smiley flung over his shoulder.

They were at the first rocks, slippery looking, seaweed-covered humps, sticking up about a foot.

Spray was beating over them, pools of water sweeping in between.

Smiley started at a run, but after a few steps he slipped, his hands plunging through thickly matted seaweed into cold water up to his elbows.

He scrambled to his feet, dripping, and went crab-wise along the reef. Anger and fear were fighting in him as the wind grew stronger, chilling his soaked arms.

Dick, silent, struggled along at his heels.

Smiley kept peering into the dark water but he could see nothing. Now seaweed, lifted by the rising tide, rose and fell from the tops of the reef. Rock after rock they scrambled past, calling, waiting, then when they caught no answer, struggling ahead. In their ears sounded the monotonous, threatening crash of the waves. Finally ahead of them was the last thin wedge of reef, the end already swept by rollers. Beyond this lay the ocean.

Dick grabbed Smiley's shoulder. "D'you see him anywhere?" he panted. "Did he get back this far?"

Smiley's eyes kept up their vain search. "No. He didn't make shore. He's somewhere out there," he ended with a gulp.

They hesitated, staring around them. Then Smiley yelled again, fear shaking his voice, "Bill, cut your kidding, Bill. C'mon out. You win. Come out!"

They tried to smother their loud breathing, to listen better, but couldn't hear for the screaming of gulls disputing a catch.

"Shut up!" Dick shouted at the circling birds.

"Come on, Dick." Smiley prodded his chum. Then as he faced the ocean again he broke off, staring. "Bill!" he roared, plunging ahead.

A pair of hands had clutched at the top of one of the nearest rocks, missed the grip and slid off. Bill, straining to lift himself, was down in the swirling water, evidently caught by something. Only his head was above the surface.

"Why didn't you sing out, you chump," Smiley yelled in relief, floundering through the last pool, Dick urging him ahead.

"I'm caught," Bill gasped, struggling to haul himself out. "My right leg's caught just above the knee. Something's holding me."

"Yeah, so we see," Smiley exulted. "Well, give us your hand and we'll get you out."

He and Dick maneuvered gingerly for footing, then, grasping Bill's dripping hands, heaved. But they couldn't raise him more than an inch or so. They straightened up and tried again. But Bill cried out and they had to let go. He was held as if in a vise.

The water, disturbed by their efforts, swirled over Bill's mouth. He gave a strangled gasp, jerking his head back.

The boys stared at each other, fear growing large in their eyes. The outer edges of the reef broke the force of the waves now, but with the rising of the tide they would be covered, and the rollers would sweep over the rocks unopposed.

"We've got to get him out," Smiley cried, galvanized into action. "That water's coming up and at high tide—" He stopped. At high tide about a foot of green water would cover the rocks. And now Bill, with the greatest effort, could barely get his head level with their tops. If they didn't get him out in a few minutes, fifteen at the most, his head would be a foot under water. For him it might as well be eighty feet.

Dismay seized them as the rollers battered the edges of the reef and curled, foaming, around them.

"Dick," Smiley cried, "keep on trying to haul him out. I'm going down to work him loose."

Dick nodded grimly and grasped Bill's soaked arms.

Smiley jerked off his windbreaker and, tossing it at Dick's feet, lowered himself into the water. It wasn't warm for late May but neither was it so cold as he had expected after a gale. Down he went, trying to see, but the water was dark and Bill, thrashing around frantically, was churning it up. Following Bill's body Smiley found that his chum's leg was caught between two rocks, one small, the other a part of a ledge.

His lungs were aching as he shot to the surface and gulped air. "Hold still," he cried, going down again, heedless of their panicky questioning looks.

He lowered himself so that he was standing on the narrow ledge directly beside Bill. He grasped the small rock, tugging, but it wouldn't yield! The water was becoming clearer now. In the dimness, growths clinging to the rocks swept in and out around Bill's body which looked like that of a dead man. Panic surged over Smiley as he struggled vainly. One man, a sailor, had been claimed by the reef. He was somewhere out there in the unknown darkness below them. What if Bill— He couldn't move the rock. He'd need tools. He couldn't do it without them.

He swam to the top and crawled onto the rocks. The water was breaking over Bill's chin as Dick, exhausted, propped him as high as he could. Their eyes pleaded for reassurance.

"What tools have you got in the car?" Smiley gasped.

Hope crowded into Bill's eyes. "Wrenches, tire pump, jack."

"How long's the jack handle?"

"About a foot."

Smiley's heart sank with the sick realization that this wouldn't do. It was far too short.

Dick was watching them both, hoping against hope that Smiley had some plan.

"We've *got* to haul him out," Smiley cried desperately, springing up. "There's no time to get help. We've *got* to, Dick!"

Dick's lips tightened. If this were the only plan! He had been struggling to lift Bill out, pulling until their arms were almost ripped out of their sockets, but the rocks still gripped fast. But Dick jumped up, too.

"We'll have to hurt you something fierce, Bill," Smiley warned.

Spray, dashing high in the air, drenched them as they waded into better position, stumbling in their efforts for speed. They reached down.

"Ready?" Smiley shot out.

Dick nodded.

But try as they would, working faster and faster against the licking waves they couldn't drag Bill free.

The cold, salt air of the sea chilled them, in spite of their efforts.

"Hey-y, out there!" A cry, battered by the wind, came faintly from behind them.

They whirled.

A man was coming toward them, running swiftly across those rocks over which they had so lately stumbled. As he came on they could see he was a young man. A young fellow in a white sweater, Craig of Black Rock High!

Unreasoning hope swept over them.

"What's the trouble?" Craig's eyes centered on Bill.

"He's caught between the rocks. His leg's caught and we can't get him loose," Smiley began.

"Can't move the rock? Tried?"

"Yes. It's no use," Smiley said swiftly. "It's too large to free without tools."

A second later Craig said, as he straightened up, "He's caught all right." He looked swiftly at the glistening sea. "He's got to have something to breathe through until we can get him out. That water'll be over his head in a few minutes." He hesitated, considering. Then, "What have you got in the car?" he demanded. "What tools?"

Smiley gave a stifled groan. Time was speeding. Was this the best Craig could do? The thin bulwark of confidence was smashed and terror overwhelmed the boy.

But Bill was answering swiftly, through chattering teeth, "Wrenches, a jack, tire pump."

"All right," Craig cut him off and turned on the boys. "Get behind him, you two. Break the force of the water. Hold him up till I get back."

"Where're you going?" Smiley shot the question even as he and Dick floundered behind Bill, hoisting him up the few precious inches. Water swept up to their waists.

But Craig didn't answer. He was already making for shore, racing across foam-licked rocks, going at a speed which threatened, if his foot slipped, to hurl him into deep water.

"What's he going to do?" Bill's voice shook, but there wasn't a whimper out of him as he still thrashed the water, trying to free himself. "What's he doing?" he demanded again, a minute later.

They saw Craig run up on the shore. They saw him take something from the car, then head for the reef again, coming at full speed. Steadily he advanced as if he were attached to some invisible pulley which drew him unerringly to them. In his hand was a rubber tube about three feet long, which Smiley recognized as part of the tire pump. "What's he going to do with that?" he thought despairingly.

"Listen, fellow," Craig caught his breath, "this is what you've got to breathe through." He pulled off his sweater, transferred his watch to one of its pockets and handed it to Smiley. "Look." He blew through the tube and found it clear. He glanced again at the waves licking around his ankles, then, taking the tube in his mouth and clipping his nose shut, he lowered himself into the water so that about a foot of the tube was above the surface.

The sound of his heavy breathing coming through the rubber and from beneath the surface of the sea sent a shiver through Smiley. He stared down at Bill whose eyes were riveted on the thin length of tube.

A minute later Craig came to the top and crawled up beside them. "O. K.," he began in a matter-of-fact way, shaking the salt water from his eyes. "Stick this in your mouth and breathe through it. Keep your nose tight shut. You'll be O. K. You'll be under a little while before we can get you out. It's up to you. You're perfectly safe as long as you don't open your mouth or get panicky. It's up to you." He stared hard at Bill. "Can you keep your nerve or are you all wind?"

Bill stared back at him. Then he nodded grimly and reached for the tube. "I can do it."

Only Smiley saw the relieved light that flashed for a second in Craig's eyes.

"You," Craig pointed to Dick. His words ripped out with the speed of machine-gun bullets. "Get back to the Tuttle farm, about a half mile from here, along the road you came. Get men. Tell 'em to bring ropes, crowbars. Get going." Dick with a frightened, indecisive look at Bill, started.

Craig turned to Smiley. "You get in to shore and get a blaze going. Oh, hey!" He cupped his hands around his mouth and shouted after Dick. "Bring coffee! Bring coffee!"

Dick's running figure turned and he yelled something they couldn't hear. "All right," Craig finished. "Make a good blaze. I'll stay out here."

Smiley looked down at Bill. "You all right, Bill?"

"Sure." Bill essayed a feeble grin.

"Go on to shore," Craig said, and then more softly, "and stay there."

Smiley searched his face but it was mask-like and he could tell nothing.

His mind was in a turmoil as he stumbled, shivering, back along the reef which was completely awash now. Spray, beating high, fell over what little of him wasn't already soaked. The monotonous crash and thunder of the waves grew louder as he neared the beach. He heard a faint clanking and saw the red roadster streak out of sight along the lane parallel to the coast. Smiley splashed across the last rocks and onto the sand, stumbling as if his head were too heavy for his legs. He turned and looked out to sea where there seemed to be only one figure moving about on the reef.

Could Bill hold out? Would he get panicky when the sea closed over his head and he knew the only thing between him and strangling death was a thin length of tube? Could he keep up the slow, steady breathing, not knowing when help would arrive? Would terror get the better of him as it grew darker? Would the cold be too much for him?

Smiley groaned through set teeth. He began tugging tremendous logs, far too big for any fire, finding relief in the physical exertion. He ran along the shore looking for kindling and driftwood. He didn't dare let his thoughts wander. He kept them firmly in one groove; he had to make a fire, a great one to dry Bill out. Craig had said he'd be all right. Though why such confidence in Craig?

The minutes plodded on.

The waves seemed to dash higher across the reef.

Smiley piled the dry kindling and driftwood beside a large rock, fumbled for a match in his waterproof box and touched it to the pile with shaking fingers. No newspapers. Kindling would have to do. The chips began to curl with a thin, reassuring crackle. The flames licked around the driftwood and fragrant smoke rose cheerfully, belying the desperate situation of the boy caught in the rocks. What was happening out there now? The tide would be high by this time. The water would be over Bill's head. Could he keep his nerve? Smiley's constant despairing glances out to sea brought him no answer.

He piled on more wood, gathered a great reserve pile, some of it still damp. He dried himself until his clothes tightened warmly and his face was burning.

The wind from the ocean whipped across the rock, bending the smoke toward the dunes.

Dick had been away a long time. What had happened?

Then into Smiley's dread and uncertainty cut a sound; a faint clanking that grew into a roar and rattle. Two cars were shooting along the lane above the shore. Now they came grinding down the wagon track, the roadster in the lead; behind it, bouncing and jouncing, a Ford. They ground to a stop with a spray of sand from the wheels. Four men carrying crowbars, pickaxes, and ropes leaped out of the car and followed Dick's mad rush.

Dick yelled, "Is he all right?"

"Hurry up!" Smiley shouted. "Hurry!"

The leader swung around to the other men, crowding close. "We'll have to go along the reef. Go easy and don't make a slip." Then, as Smiley and Dick darted into the water he yelled, "Come back, you fellows. 'Nough out there as 'tis. Stay ashore!"

He splashed carefully out onto the rocks, watching each step.

The others crowded past Smiley and Dick who were hesitating, not knowing whether to stay or go ahead regardless. The last man flung over his shoulder, "There's coffee to make. Do that!"

Steadily the rescuers were moving along the wave-beaten rocks toward the indistinct figure far out. One man slipped. The others swung around to make sure that he was all right, then started ahead again.

"Oh," Dick groaned, "if they'd only get a move on!"

"Come on, Dick." Smiley couldn't watch the tantalizing progress any longer. "We'll make that coffee."

They got it, in a limp paper bag, from the car. "Where's the pot?" Smiley demanded, his voice unnaturally loud.

"Here." Dick banged out a tin pail. "That was the first thing handy."

Smiley grabbed it and they ran back to the fire, dumped in the coffee and with water from a stream in the woods got it started, setting the pail on the rock where the leaping flames could heat it.

"They've reached them!" he shouted suddenly, pointing. A cluster of men, indistinguishable, was out at the reef's end.

"Smiley," Dick, whitefaced, stared at him across the fire and voiced his own fear, "do you think they'll get him out? In time?"

"Sure!" Smiley grabbed a piece of driftwood and began stirring the coffee around, sloshing it against the side of the pail. Some of it spilled, hissing, into the flames.

"They're a long time," Dick said, finally.

Silence.

"Got any mugs or anything for them to drink out of?"

Dick shook his head. He drew a shuddering breath, then leaned over, inspecting the coffee with an interest he did not feel. "Looks kinda muddy," he declared shakily. "Thick."

Smiley straightened up as the mixture came to a boil. "Let it stand now," he said, shoving it farther back on the stone.

They went down to the shore where the waves came surging in, then with a long-drawn hiss, sucking out.

"Smiley," Dick blurted, "I'm going to Bill. I can't stick here any longer."

A faint cry drifted in to them. What was it? Was Bill safe?

They sped farther along the beach to get a better view. Then they yelled, shouting and pounding each other. Bill was out! They could see him vaguely, as the men moved apart, a sagging figure supported by Craig.

"Boy!" They darted for the fire. "Build it up!"

"Get that coffee ready!"

Dick rammed a stick through the pail handle and set it in the sand. Then quickly wrapping his hands in the sleeves of his windbreaker, he lifted the steaming pail and, blowing, tasted it.

The men were making for shore quickly, a thin line, with Craig and Bill bringing up the rear. The boys raced to meet them. The men splashed onto the sand, talking excitedly. "When I dug my bar in that time," one declared, "I said, 'If this don't do the trick, nuthin' will.' "

"Kid's got plenty of nerve, down under water like that!"

"It was Craig saved him, though, keeping his courage up, keeping his blood circ'latin'."

Bill and Craig were nearing shore now, Bill leaning heavily on the young coach.

"Bill!" The boys splashed through the shallow water to him. "Bill!" they yelled, helping to steady his stumbling footsteps. "Bill!" They pounded him, unable to find words.

"He's got to dry off, fellows," Craig advised. "Get him over to the fire."

"Come on, Bill."

They helped him over, shoving into the group of men who were crowding around the flames, their clothes steaming. They had discovered the coffee and were passing it around, tilting their heads to get the smoking, rank tasting stuff.

"Give him some of that." Smiley reached for the pail and helped Bill lift it.

So far Bill had been able to give only weak croaks to their exciting questions and they watched him anxiously.

He managed a swallow, then choked. "That's your coffee, all right, Smiley," he wheezed hoarsely. "I'd know it anywhere."

The boys went off in yells. Bill was O. K.

By now the men were warm and dried out. Everybody looked at Bill. He tried to thank them but they brushed it aside with grins of embarrassment. "'Twarn't us," they declared, looking at Craig.

"Better get him home to bed," the young coach advised, cutting off any praise. "He'll have pneumonia."

The men agreed, nodding solemnly. Then the leader said, "Guess we'd better be getting home too. Won't have a birdseed for dinner if we don't."

With handshakes and congratulations all around they got into their machine, and were off with a roar. They'd have much to talk about for months to come; how the visitin' boy had been caught on Destruction Reef at risin' tide, how Jim Craig had come along, and so on and so on.

With Craig's help, Smiley and Dick doused the fire and then got Bill installed in the car, covered with all the available windbreakers and sweaters, including Craig's. They heard Bill say to the young coach — "as much for you some day."

They couldn't catch Craig's answer, but he gave a laugh and slapped Bill on the back. Then with a "Good luck" he started down the beach, drawing a pipe from his pocket and tipping the water from it.

"Gee, Bill," Dick began as he crowded in beside his chum, "you sure gave us a scare. We thought you were a goner."

"Would have been," Bill managed in a hoarse whisper, as he settled himself in the seat, his legs high on the dashboard, "if it hadn't been for Jim."

"Jim? Oh, Craig."

"Sure. Boy, what a prince he is. Know what I'm going to do tomorrow?" Bill's voice was a harsh croak. "I'm going down there when he's coaching that team of apes, and apologize to him before the lot of them."

"I don't think he's the kind of fellow who'd want that," Smiley objected.

"Maybe not, but I've got to do something to square myself. Gosh, how could I have been such a mutt? How could I?" Bill shook his head bewilderedly. "Gee, if I could only do something for him. You know," he broke off, "there seems to be something worrying him, hanging over him, that he can't shake off. Did you hear anything about him, Smiley?"

Smiley shifted into second. "No. I asked at the Post Office but Pop McIntyre didn't know much about him."

They swung into the lane leading toward Black Hill and stared down at the shore.

There was Craig, a lonely figure looking out to sea.

They were silent for a few minutes as they sped along, then Bill, saying something he was to repeat many times in the next few hours, spoke, "You fellows mark my words. I'm not going to be satisfied until I make it up to him for what he did for me today. For everything." He stared unseeingly for a minute at the swiftly passing pines, then the old familiar grin broke over his face, but this time there was no trace of bravado about it. "You fellows were pretty splendid too," he floundered.

"Yeah? What'd we do?" Smiley laughed that off. Then, "Say, fellows," he went on, "how about our coming down here early tomorrow at low tide and getting a real look at that wreck?"

"O. K." Dick seconded swiftly.

They waited.

"You bet," Bill boomed. "Nothing I'd like better."

CHAPTER III

About seven-thirty that night Miss Jennie Adams, Smiley's aunt, fastened her eyes sternly on the bulky figure propped up in the four-poster bed. "Now, Wilfred," she demanded for the tenth time, "are you sure you feel all right?"

Bill glared at Smiley and Dick grinning at him from the foot of the bed. "Yes'm, Miss Adams," he croaked.

Aunt Jennie shook her head dismally, then with a final undecided look said, "Well, then, I'll just drop over to Miss Tibbett's for a second. You, Smiley, be sure to go down after his medicine at eight o'clock. Doctor said 'twould be ready by then."

Aunt Jennie turned the lamp wick down a trifle, then lowered the open window a bit. "Cold enough to freeze a body in here," she declared, as she went out into the hall.

Chip-Chip, her mongrel pup, who followed her everywhere, bounded from Smiley's knees and stretched his way after her.

"Gee, Smiley," Bill protested, "I hate to give your aunt all this trouble."

Smiley laughed. "Aunt Jen loves it," he asserted confidently. "There she goes now," as the back door closed firmly, "to tell her friends all about it."

They looked through the swaying, primly starched curtains and made out Miss Adams, with Chip bouncing ahead of her, picking her way across the moonlit meadow.

Behind her lay the gleaming waters of Black Hill Bay where, near shore, her motor boat rocked at its mooring. The scattered lights of the village, off to the left, made a yellow semi-circle of dotted lines around the head of the bay and, towering high like some gloomy guardian, was the dark mass of Black Hill, its rounded top beneath the North Star.

Dick shifted suddenly and pulled out his watch. "Say," he exclaimed, "it's time for the scores."

"That's right." Smiley got to his feet and crossed to the radio. "It's on WTZ, isn't it?" Setting the dials on the correct numbers he snapped the switch. Out of the loudspeaker came a faint, rasping voice which gradually strengthened.

"Those are all the scores in the National League," the announcer reported. A rustling of paper.

"Now they'll say whether Clinton or Lake Forest won," Bill wheezed confidently, settling back against the pillows.

The unknown voice began again. "There was only one game played in the American League today, New York at Philadelphia. The Yanks won, 3-2, by virtue of a home run by the Babe in the sixth inning. Batteries for the Yanks, Johnson and Dickey. For the A's, Grove, Earnshaw and Cochrane. That concludes our sports talk for the day, ladies and gentlemen."

"Oh, pshaw," Bill growled. "Don't they think people want to know whether Clinton or Lake Forest won? Don't they think people are interested in which one plays us for the championship of our state?"

"Folks back home in Westbury, yes," Smiley answered, "but maybe people tuned in on New York can live without knowing."

"Fine service I call it anyhow." Bill was unappeased.

"Well," Smiley drew a chair in front of the radio and said over his shoulder, "when I go down after your medicine, interesting invalid, I'll see if the Portland paper has it."

His fingers were poised over the dial when a new voice broke in, "We interrupt the program at this point to give you a message from Chief of Police McAndrews. The authorities of Great Barrens Prison report the escape of Stewart Sheldon, sometime late yesterday. Description follows; fifty-six years old, six feet tall, heavy build, gray hair, dark blue eyes. Anyone having information regarding Stewart Sheldon communicate at once with the police or this station."

"H'm," Dick commented, "escaped from Great Barrens. Not many get out of there. Some stunt!"

Bill scoffed. "Now why couldn't they have taken that time to tell us whether Clinton or Lake Forest won?"

"Hold your horses." Smiley looked at the clock on the mantel. "I'll be going down to the village in a few minutes. Who is this Sheldon? Do you know anything about him? Name seems familiar."

Dick frowned. "Seems to me," he said slowly, "he was some wealthy stockbroker or something."

"Or something!" Bill derided. "Stewart Sheldon was a broker. His partner was murdered and he was accused. Though he claimed he was innocent he was tried and convicted. The Governor granted several delays in order that Sheldon's friends might find a missing witness who could clear him. But they couldn't locate the man and Sheldon was going to the chair next week. How's that for a memory? And all correct, too."

Smiley looked at Dick and shook his head sorrowfully, "Bill's reformation didn't last."

"Huh? Oh!" Bill grinned cheerfully. "Well,

leopard's spots," he said. Then thoughtfully, "Wonder what Craig's doing now."

Smiley stood up, stretching. "Probably sitting beside the phone, waiting for you to call." He ducked Bill's pillow, tossed it back. "I'm going down now, Dick. You coming?"

Dick yawned comfortably. "No. I'll stay here and be entertained. You go along without me."

"Don't forget that paper." Bill's hoarse voice followed Smiley as he took his cap from the rack and let himself out the back door.

He walked swiftly down the silent main street. Here and there in a little house set well back from the road a light shone in an upper window. The inhabitants of Black Hill were preparing for bed.

Smiley's feet crunched along the gravel sidewalk. Tall trees lined the path. The moon, across which clouds drifted, thrust their huge shadows over the roadway. From the swamps to Smiley's left came the monotonous, high-pitched calling of the frogs. Absentmindedly he imitated their cry as he went along. "This has been some day," he thought, and shivered as he remembered what might so easily have happened. He passed the high school, its deserted playing field ablaze with lights as the electricians tested their lamps in preparation for the next night's game. He went by the locked Post Office. Ahead of him was the drug store, brightly lighted.

A roar of laughter swept out to him as he ran up the creaking steps and shoved open the rusty screen door. A group of loungers, still grinning at some joke, was sitting by the crackling, pot-bellied stove. They twisted around and gave Smiley a glance as he went over to the counter, then shifted their attention back to the speaker, a red-faced youngster, laughing, waiting for the applause to subside. He was leaning back against the showcase, flanked by five or six companions. He towered above them, husky farmer boys though they were. His broad shoulders threatened to burst his sweater with its flaring letters BLACK HILL ACADEMY. He leaned forward a little and went on, his face grim now, set in an angry scowl, "And did I tell him where he got off at? Trying to tell me how to play baseball. Me! Huh!" He shook his head incredulously and his mates nodded in approval.

Smiley grinned to himself as he recognized the fellow from the morning, Cole, whooping it up again.

The clerk, a nervous little man in a streaked alpaca coat too large for him, hurried from the rear. He peered at Smiley over his gold-rimmed spectacles, then, recognizing him, wheeled and trotted back to the rear room which a faded sign proclaimed PRESCR PT ON DEPT.

Cole was off again, his strident voice storming at his audience. "I tell you," he roared, pounding the counter so that the bottles trembled, "he's a four-flusher. Why, I've forgotten more baseball than he'll ever know. He wouldn't dare stand up to me!"

The druggist's assistant, worried for the safety of his bottles, shook his head dismally as he wrapped Smiley's package. "His father's selectman, very influential man," he muttered in explanation. He gave one more wretched glance at Cole, debating whether or not to protest, then apparently deciding against it rang up the cash register and retreated.

Smiley turned as Cole, working himself to fever pitch stormed, "And what's more I tell you Craig's a cheap coward!"

Smiley's face was grim as he laid the medicine gently on the counter and walked over to Cole. "And I tell *you,*" he said, "you're a cheap liar!"

A chair banged to the floor as its occupant moved swiftly toward the door. Cole jerked up, his mouth open in amazement. He towered over Smiley's five feet eleven as he glared down at him, seething with inarticulate rage.

"And listen, kid," Smiley went on softly, tapping Cole on the chest, "you'd better stop imitating a movie villain. You'll burst a blood vessel."

Cole spluttered, his face purpling, "You— you—"

His friends moved close behind him. The flaring

gas light made their faces all lights and shadows as, with heads thrust forward, they waited.

But their leader seemed unable to get going. He gulped, shifting his footing uncertainly, clenching and unclenching his broad fists. He was big enough, powerful enough to match Smiley easily, but he hesitated, and the longer he delayed the less dangerous he was.

"I don't scare worth a cent," Smiley offered grimly.

A crafty look came into Cole's narrowed eyes and he forced a thin-lipped grin. "Oh," he snarled contemptuously, "I wouldn't bother with this mutt. He's just an outsider."

Smiley gave a smothered sigh of relief. "That's an easy way to get out of it." He laughed and picking up his medicine faced the clerk who had reappeared and whose nervous frightened fingers were fluttering along the edge of the scarred counter. "Where can I get the latest paper?" he asked.

"D-d-down the street at Miss Aunders." He pointed vaguely with a trembling hand. "Less'n she's shet up by now."

"Thanks." Smiley gave a last look at Cole and laughed again.

As he stepped onto the moonlight flooded porch he heard behind him a bull-like roar, "I'll get you for this!"

Smiley knew it would be the better part of valor to make for his aunt's without delay but he was determined that they weren't going to scare him out of getting his paper. He faced away from home and started down the street. The few shops he passed were locked for the night; the A & P, plumbing shop and notions. Across the way was a little stationery store, two oblongs of light shining through its door. As Smiley crossed to it, one of these oblongs was blotted out as a shade was rolled up.

"Hey, wait!" He broke into a run, the change jingling in his pocket as he raced up the narrow wooden steps. "Wait a minute!"

A timid head bobbed up above the top of the second, half-rolled shade.

"Paper? Can I get a Portland paper?"

He heard a swift scurrying to and fro, then silence. He looked swiftly behind him, but the street was still deserted. Then the door in front of him grudgingly creaked open and he whisked inside. Quickly he shot the shade the rest of the way to the top, then lifted aside the corner and peered out. He gave a sudden breath as he counted six or seven figures come out of the lighted drug store, point toward Aunders' store and melt into the shadows. Now he was in for it.

He straightened up and turned to Miss Aunders. She was staring at him goggle-eyed, one hand delicately clutching her throat, the other frantically signalling to someone above stairs. But as she recognized Smiley she gave a gusty, relieved sigh.

"It's you! Mercy me, how you scared me!" She raised her voice and called toward the stairs, "It's all right now, Pa! It's only Miss Adams' nevew."

A grunt from the stairway, and looking up, Smiley saw a pair of skinny, nightshirt-clad legs loom into view.

"No, Pa!" Miss Aunders shouted, scurrying toward him, as the cautious descent still continued. "It's all right. You can go back to bed! Pa can't hear a mite without his trumpet," she grimaced to Smiley.

"Eh? What say?" The old fellow halted, peering down at them. Then he turned, and with more gruntings made his way to the upper floor.

"I swan," Miss Aunders exclaimed, whisking a Portland paper from under the counter, "I thought you must be one of those men from the swamp gang. That's why I sent for Pa."

Smiley paid for the paper and wrapped it around the medicine. He might need to have his hands as free as possible before he reached his aunt's.

Outside he waited for a second in the shadow of the building, searching the quiet street. His eyes followed the line of low, small stores. Beyond them lay the little houses of the village, each one some distance from its neighbors. Great trees lined the gravel walk and in their shadows any number of skulkers might lie concealed.

There was no breath of wind to stir the branches, no sound but the monotonous cry of frogs from the swamp.

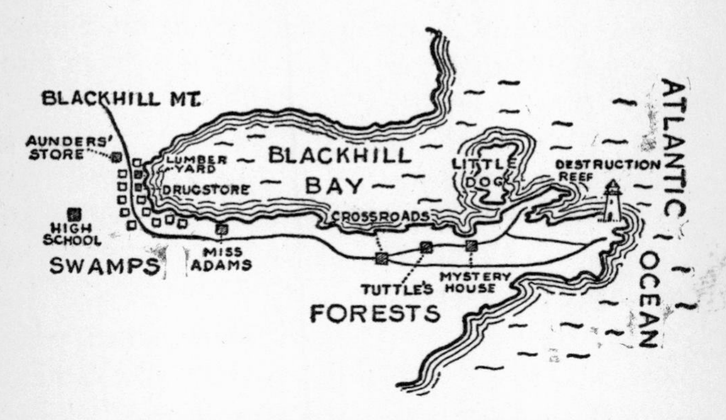

Smiley thought swiftly over the lay of the land to see if there were any way to avoid running the gantlet which he was sure lay for him just beyond the stores.

"Could I skirt the swamp, then cut across to Aunt Jen's?" he thought, but decided against that. The trail through the swamp was too dangerous even in daylight and for one who knew the country well.

Then suddenly Smiley grinned as another plan came to him. His aunt's back meadow bordered on the bay. He knew that down by the lumberyard directly opposite where he stood now, a rowboat was always beached. He'd borrow that and row home!

Seeing nothing at all suspicious he left the shelter of the store and cut toward the lumberyard. But halfway across the street a sense of uneasiness assailed him. He slowed, unable to account for it. He swiftly identified all the night sounds, then he got it! There it came again! In front of him, down by the lumberyard, sounded the call of a frog, but too high-pitched, more excited than any real frog ever was.

From behind Smiley came an answering cry. He swerved suddenly and instead of continuing toward the water went along the sidewalk, back the way he had come. Clearly his path to the boat was blocked.

He moved along unhurriedly, apparently suspecting nothing, yet with each sense keyed. His eyes darted ahead to every clump of shadowy bushes. He could have walked in the center of the street but that would have told them at once that he knew something was up. All they'd have had to do was swoop out at him and that'd be just too bad, six or seven against one.

The shadows were deceiving: they had him worried. He'd center on one, only to have it resolve itself into an ashcan or pile of boxes. In the meantime he was approaching the real danger.

A plan was taking shape in his mind, but he'd have

to locate the ambush or it could never work. He had passed the last store now. There was still about a quarter mile ahead of him. It'd come any minute now.

The cry of the frog kept following him. It came more frequently, no nearer, but surely and steadily. Evidently it was the signal that he was coming.

Smiley grunted angrily. What'd they think he was? Some dope to be fooled by their travelling frog? He tightened his grip on the medicine. Apparently they had him, if he couldn't detect their hiding-place, but he'd get in a couple of good cracks with the bottle before it smashed against some head. He went warily along. The moon slid behind a bank of clouds and he hurried faster. He might be able to make the next dark blotch of bushes and slip away. Then the moon sailed out again and he slowed down, gritting his teeth.

Now he was going through a bright patch of moonlight, passing by a stretch of picket fence. There was no sound but his own crunching footsteps and the calling of his trailer. Then suddenly his aching eyes detected something.

About fifty feet ahead of him, the distance shortening every minute, he'd have to pass two giant trees whose shadows lay across the road. There were strange bulges in those shadows. Now one shifted a bit!

Smiley's heart leaped. He was nearing the gate in the fence. As he came directly opposite it he bent over as if fumbling with a shoelace. Through the crook of his arm he looked behind him in time to spy a dark blur leap into the shelter of a tree.

That instant Smiley shoved at the gate. It swung open and he was inside, crouching in the protection of a thick bush.

For a minute everything was still. The frog had stopped its calling. From his position Smiley watched alternately his back track, where nothing moved, and ahead, where the ones waiting for him were huddled ready to leap out. The seconds dragged. Those in ambush were becoming more anxious and Smiley thought he could hear them whisper. Then he caught a soft stealthy crunching as someone passed his hiding-place, moving warily. It was Cole.

On hands and knees Smiley crawled forward and edged his head around the gate.

Cole was nearing the ambush now. Nearer. He was almost up to it!

Smiley sprang to his feet and shouted, "Get him, gang! *Get him!*"

Like shots from a gun five racing figures plunged from the shadows, bending low. They hurled themselves on their leader, tackling him around the knees, bringing him down with vicious body punches, leaping on him, pummelling him unmercifully.

He screamed like a stuck pig, howling, "*Lemme up! You fools!* It's *me. It's me. Ow-w! !*"

Grinning from ear to ear, Smiley sprang out of the gate and swiftly circled the heaving, grunting pile, sprouting with flailing arms and legs. The heap crashed into trees, then rolled the other way, banging into the wooden fence.

The way to his aunt's was open before Smiley. He swung around standing in the moonlight where they'd be sure to recognize him. "Hooray!" he shouted, bending down and watching them, hands planted lightly on his knees.

The squirming mass disentangled.

"Hooray!" he yelled again. "Three cheers for Cole, the strategist!"

Then casting dignity to the winds he tore down the road, hearing for the first few minutes the pounding feet of his already winded pursuers. He thundered up his aunt's back steps and wheeled around, panting.

The night was serene. The stars blinked on an empty street. From the swamps came the high, unhurried calling of real frogs.

"Oh, boy!" Smiley roared, stumbling weakly into the kitchen.

"What on earth's the matter with you?"

Aunt Jennie was setting a dish of water before Chip, who barked disapprovingly as she straightened up. "Smiley Adams, where's that medicine?"

"Here, Aunt Jen." He handed it to her. "Come on in and get a load of this."

He made for the bedroom, still chuckling, where Dick and Bill looked up from a game of checkers.

"Oh, ow-w," he gasped, launching himself into one of his aunt's antique armchairs. "This's rich! Listen. You know that fellow Cole?" He paused for breath.

"That big windtrap on Craig's team? Yeah." Bill nodded, quietly lifting his two men and Dick's seven from the checkerboard and dropping them into their box. "Well?"

"Well —" Smiley began.

From out in the kitchen came a bang, Chip's frenzied barking and Aunt Jen's mounting scream.

"It's a gun!" Smiley roared, leaping from the chair, Dick after him and Bill, flinging aside the covers, bringing up the rear.

Aunt Jen stood there in the center of the floor, a dripping, fizzing medicine bottle in her spattered fingers. She was staring at the spreading pool at which Chip was sniffing inquiringly.

"What kind of medicine's this?" she cried, shoving Chip back. "When I took off the string the cork popped out and it swam over everything! You go right back —"

"Oh, gee, Aunt Jen, I'm sorry. That was my

fault," Smiley confessed. "I was running and I guess it got a bit shook up."

"Well, I swan. Back you go for more. I'll phone him to make up another prescription and you march right over after it. Come along."

The boys followed meekly, struggling to control their laughter. Back in the bedroom Smiley started with much gusto his story of Cole and the night's happenings. Aunt Jen's voice came clear and strong from the phone. "What do you mean keeping me waiting so long? No matter if you were in bed. You shouldn't be. Now I've got to have that medicine made up again. I've a very sick person on my hands and I must have it. I'll send my nephew for it."

"Listen, Smiley," Dick cut in, "if you're going back again I'm going with you. Those fellows may be hanging around yet."

"I'm in on this," Bill declared. "Boy, I'm wrathy. I'll pop that fellow on sight. The cheek of him saying Craig's a coward. And that he doesn't know baseball. Why—say," he remembered suddenly. "What about the Clinton-Lake Forest game?"

"Outside." Smiley went back to the kitchen for the discarded medicine-stained newspaper. "But there's nothing about the game in it," he reported, riffling through it. "Nope," he decided finally, "we'll just have to wait until tomorrow, I guess."

Bill growled in disgust.

"But here's about that escape." Smiley settled back in the armchair.

Under the heading:

STEWART SHELDON

WHO ESCAPED FROM THE DEATH HOUSE AT GREAT BARRENS PRISON

was the man's picture.

Dick leaned over Smiley's shoulder. "He's a fine looking man, isn't he?" he commented.

"Sure," Bill interrupted impatiently, "didn't I tell you he was a wealthy broker? He'd have to make a good appearance."

"Not that." Dick wasn't satisfied. "He doesn't look like a criminal. There's something about his face—"

"Ugh! There's something about a rose!" Bill growled. "Say, hand me that sports section. You two've probably missed the part about the game after all."

Smiley tossed him the second part while he and Dick went on reading about Sheldon.

Aunt Jennie came in with an armful of windbreakers and sweaters. "Here are your things.

They're all dried out now and I won't have them cluttering up my kitchen. Here's yours, Dick, Wilfred. Does this belong to you, Smiley?"

He glanced up. Aunt Jen was holding a thick white sweater. "No," he said, surprised. "That's not mine. I never saw it before."

"Craig's," Bill said.

"Oh, yes, that's right." Smiley laid down the paper. "He lent it to Bill this afternoon. Toss, Aunt Jen."

"I will not." She folded it across a chair and, with a glance at Bill again searching through the paper, said, "And don't you forget to go after that medicine in half an hour."

"O. K." As his aunt closed the door Smiley tipped his chair far over on one side and reached for the sweater. He gripped it and dragged it toward him. As it slid from the chair something dropped from the pocket with a thud.

"Oh, Jeerusalem," he whistled, springing up. "His watch! Have I busted it?" Swiftly he went down on hands and knees and lifted the watch, a thin sliver of platinum. "What a beauty," he admired, opening it carefully. "What luck!" The crystal was unbroken.

"There's a picture in it," Dick declared, reaching over and turning it around.

"Yeah." Smiley looked at the snapshot pasted in

the case and read the engraving, *To Jim. From Dad.* "Guess that's his father."

"Let's see it," Bill demanded. "Oh, boy, that must have cost plenty of mazuma."

"Five hundred at least," Dick hazarded. "Don't you think so, Smiley?"

Smiley nodded, his face puzzled. Then suddenly he leaned over and took the open watch from Bill's admiring hands. He stared at the snapshot.

"What's the matter with you?" they demanded.

Smiley's eyes shifted to them unseeingly. Quickly he grabbed the front page of the newspaper, straightened it out, spreading it in the yellow circle of lamplight.

"Say, what— Are you crazy?" Bill cried.

"Look!" Smiley whispered, laying the open watch on the Portland paper so that the snapshot and the newspaper picture of Stewart Sheldon were side by side. "They're the same man!"

Bill dragged the paper closer to the light. "It's his picture. It's Craig's father!"

In the sudden silence they stared from one to the other.

"What'll we do?"

"Do?" Bill flared. "Keep it to ourselves of course. Don't let anyone know that Craig's father—"

"Shut up!" Smiley leaped from the bed and raced for the open window.

From the porch outside was the swift scurry of running footsteps. Smiley flung the window high. He caught sight of a figure speeding across the lawn.

"Cole!" he gritted, flashing around to Dick and Bill, crowding close. Then, realization dawning, "What'd he hear?"

CHAPTER IV

"AND WHAT'LL Cole do?" Smiley rapped out, slamming down the creaking window.

"Blab!"

"That's sure," Dick agreed.

"Then we've got to get word to Craig, quick!" Bill grabbed for his socks. His shadow leaped, enormous, across the flowered wallpaper as he bent over.

"*You're* not going." Smiley crowded him rapidly toward the bed. "Don't be a darn fool, Bill. You'd get pneumonia."

"I *am* going!" Bill shouted resolutely, shaking off Smiley's hold and backing into the table. "You think I'd stay here after Craig saved my life? What kind d'you think I am?"

"Ugh," Dick derided, reaching out and steadying the teetering kerosene lamp. "Don't be heroic. Smiley and I'll go down there and warn him. That's enough. He—"

"Now wait a minute," Smiley broke in. "You stay put, Bill." He looked at Dick. "This may turn out to be no pink tea. An escaped murderer's liable to be desperate. You sure you want to get into it?" He asked merely to salve his conscience; he was eager to have Dick with him in whatever lay ahead.

"Sure," Dick said. "And we certainly owe it to Craig."

"You bet," Bill seconded, strangely acquiescent in not going himself.

Smiley grinned. "That's fine. Let's go then. Things have been tame for too long!"

From the mantel clock came a preliminary wheeze, then a soft slow chiming of nine mellow notes.

As promptly as a cuckoo, Aunt Jen clicked her door open and appeared down the dark hall, her yellow wrapper tied with a thick cord, the light from her room streaming out behind her. "Time to go for that medicine, Smiley," she called firmly, waiting. Chip collapsed with a doggy sigh at her feet.

In the bedroom the boys froze; here was a complication.

Smiley's eyes darted from Bill out to his aunt and back to Dick. "You come, Dick," he muttered. Then, aloud, "We're just going, Aunt Jen."

"What're you going to do?" Bill demanded under his breath as the other two struggled into their windbreakers. Smiley grabbed up Craig's sweater and watch.

"Get down to Craig's. Tell him what we've found out, and that Cole knows, too."

"D'you think his father's down there?" Bill shuffled rapidly after them to the door.

"Don't know."

Dick and Smiley started down the hall, full drive. "All set, Aunt Jen," Smiley assured her.

"Hypocrites," Bill wheezed to himself. There was a strange grin on his face as he turned swiftly back into his room.

"See here!" Outside, Aunt Jen halted Smiley and Dick. "No running this time, mind you."

"No. We're going to take the car," Smiley promised, as he passed.

"The car?" his aunt echoed. "What on earth for?" Her voice was edged with doubt.

"Well—" Smiley was becoming mired. "We don't want to meet Cole and his crowd again. They may still be after me."

"Nonsense! What are you afraid of?"

It was fully five minutes later that Smiley finally convinced his aunt that it would be better if they took the roadster, and he and Dick closed the kitchen door after them and ran down the back steps.

"What were you trying to tap out with your ring?" asked Dick. Morse code, wasn't it?"

"Yes. I was trying to tell you to say we'd save a

lot of time if we took the car. But I guess my Morse is a bit rusty."

"'Rusty' is mild," Dick agreed.

Their eyes darted swiftly over the back meadow with its gloomy border of trees and swaying bushes. It was darker now; rapidly the moon was clouding over.

Satisfied that the way was clear, they hurried across the gravel driveway to the garage. Suddenly, as they crunched along, Dick said, "Hear anything ahead to the left?"

Smiley halted, pretending to have difficulty with the buttons of his windbreaker. "No." He listened. "What'd it sound like?"

"Like something running past the bushes."

"May be Cole's bunch," Smiley muttered, slowly starting forward. "Watch out they're not waiting for us there in the garage."

Warily they scraped back the wooden doors. The roadster stood in the center of the oil-streaked floor. The black night pressed against the grimy window panes. One window was partly open: torn spider webs flapped in and out.

"That window wasn't open when we put the car in." Dick pointed at it.

Alarmed, their eyes searched the garage, but nothing seemed disturbed.

"There's nothing here," Smiley decided loudly, kicking aside the broken link he had nipped from the tire chain that afternoon. But he was nervous as he jumped into the roadster and snapped on the ignition.

"Hurry up!" Dick was waiting to close the garage doors. His eyes flashed uneasily to the half-platform over his head, with its concealing shadows, then to the open doors beside him leading out to the windy darkness.

"Battery's on the bum," Smiley cried impatiently when, after a dozen attempts, the motor finally caught and he switched on the headlights. A yellow glow sprang up on the rear wall. Simultaneously, Dick, scrambling into the roadster, banged the door shut.

The tire chains bit, slowly at first, then faster and faster into the soft gravel.

"I don't see anything," Dick reported, sliding down in the chill leather seat, as they backed through the patch of light from Bill's open window and shot into the dark main street. "Something funny about that garage window, though."

Smiley headed in the direction of the coast; immediately they felt the increased force of the wind as it swept by them.

"We'll get that medicine on our way back. We can't delay a minute now. Storm's coming," Smiley said, as he tightened the vibrating windshield.

The village street ended abruptly a few hundred feet farther on, and they turned into a black country lane. The going was soft and the top layer of mud curved, squishing, from the wheels as the chains began their rhythmic gripping.

The sky was now almost completely overcast, a dim top to the night surrounding them. On either side, dark meadows were slipping by. To the left, for a little while they caught the faint blur of the bay.

They neared the forest, a blank black wall into which the headlights showed the lane disappearing. As they crawled between the first trees and it grew instantly colder, Smiley snapped the headlights to "Full."

"Those lights are dim," he muttered.

They crept along the bottom of a world of darkness, only a feeble glimmer from their lights pointing the way. The beams shone faintly on tossing bushes, bent almost double by the increasing wind, and on huge tree trunks crowding close behind them.

Above their heads, the boys could hear, but not see, the creaking tree-tops, their blackness merging with the sky.

"Is this the way we came this morning?" Dick questioned doubtfully.

"Yes."

"Seems different."

It *was* different from the daylight. Then they

had sped, jouncing, along the narrow lane, their chain banging against the fender noisily, as though they were lords of creation. The great stretches of huge pines and beeches, hiding unseen life, had seemed just part of the scenery, lifeless, unaware of them. But now, with the night, it was as though the forest had stirred, becoming alive, and were raising a barrier against them, to protect its own. The on-coming storm, the wind blowing them back, the heavy darkness; all shouted a warning.

"Say," Dick cried suddenly as Smiley swerved to the right, "you nearly hit that rock. These lights are getting fierce."

Smiley hunched forward over the wheel, as though trying by main strength to increase the force of the headlights. He was going more slowly now. The lane was little more than a muddy wagon track, a strip of grass blowing in the center. Hissing bushes, only faintly pricked into reality, scraped the sides of the car. The wind swept into the folded-back top of the roadster, whipping it, rattling, in and out.

For what seemed hours they struggled along the inky track. As they came nearer the coast, it blew colder. Smiley gripped the wheel with chill fingers, and Dick slid down in the seat, his hands thrust into his sweater sleeves.

They passed the abandoned farm, the clearing a break in the forest wall.

Anxiously, Smiley watched the fast fading lights, flickering up and down with the slow jouncing and creaking of the car.

They crawled by the wind-swept crossroad, with its weather-beaten sign tumbled in the waving grass —2 MI. DESTRUCTION REEF LIGHT-HOUSE—then bore steadily to the left as the track plunged deeper into the forest. The waves sounded louder now, with a steady, monotonous crash.

"We're near there," Smiley decided in relief, peering ahead, and shifting to low as they prepared to crawl over a shoulder of tip-tilted rock. "Tuttle's farm is about a quarter mile away, then Craig's is half a mile beyond that."

As they ground up the rise, the headlights faded. The blackness ahead rushed closer, pushing back the feeble glimmer.

"Listen, Dick." Smiley's eyes were glued to the faint wavering track, lighted dimly only a few feet ahead of them. "See if there's a flash in that pocket, or any matches. These lights won't last."

Dick fumbled in the side pocket. "No—nothing here but some greasy rags." He rubbed his hands, smelling of oil, together. "And a few—*there they go!*"

The headlights had given one last struggling flicker and blacked out. With a rush, darkness enveloped the car. The breakers thundered louder;

the wind ripped through the tree-tops. Everything held at bay seemed ready, waiting to overpower them.

The chain links clanked slower and slower as the car settled to a stop.

"Well," Dick grunted, struggling up, "looks as if we walk."

Smiley snapped the switch from "Full" to "Dim," on and off, but it was no use. He straightened, banging his head against the steering wheel.

"Confound it," he growled. "Say, why leave everything to me? Why don't you think of something?" He rubbed his head, scowling at the indistinct blur beside him that was Dick.

A bush, whipped by the wind, scratched the side of the car.

"Say," Dick questioned, his voice raised above the noise of the oncoming storm, "I thought I heard something moving out there. Are there any animals in these woods?"

"Sure." Smiley's answer came muffled as he leaned over, trying to find some loose connection, hoping that some wire was disconnected. "There are bucks up in the hills; bears were killed here last year; nobody knows what's in the swamps."

Dick was staring ahead trying to pierce the night. A sudden thought struck him and he said nervously, "There may be something else."

"What?"

"A murderer!"

Smiley felt a chill shoot along his spine. He jerked up, anger at Dick surging over him. "What're you trying to do?" he demanded. "Afraid?"

"Not too comfortable," Dick admitted, from the dark.

"Ugh," Smiley grunted in disgust, "we're no kids, to be scared at nothing." But he too listened, striving to separate any sounds of nearby movement from the noise of the wind. "Well," he began quickly, as though to cry down his fear, "one of us has got to stay here with the car while the other goes to Tuttle's for a lantern."

He sensed Dick's swing around to him.

"Why can't both of us go?" Dick asked.

"Because—" Angrily, Smiley caught the nervous, unreasoning tremor in his own voice. "There's a tough gang working in the swamps. Some of them might get down this far and make off with the bus."

"No light."

"Down here men always carry flashes when they're out at night. That'd be enough to steer her somewhere and hide her 'til morning."

"Well, lock it."

"Can't get the key out of the switch."

Their voices came, disembodied, battered by the wind as they sat there arguing, becoming more angry as the elements keyed to a higher pitch, heralding the storm.

"Do you want to go or stay?" Smiley's voice was edged.

But Dick didn't answer. He wasn't listening to him.

"What's the matter with you?" Smiley snapped.

Dick shoved back against him. "There's something moving out there," he cried. "Hear it? Listen!" His groping hand tightened on Smiley's arm. *"What's that?"*

Seemingly from underneath the car came the noise of a heavy body moving. The roadster swayed, its springs sagging and groaning as something crashed against the back.

With yells, Smiley and Dick sprang up, facing the way they had come, their shoulders whipped by the wind. Their eyes strained ahead into the night, black as a tinker's pot, trying to see from which side attack would leap.

Then, from directly in front of them, came a muffled, gasping roar, mounting in crescendo, "aaAACHOO! aaAACHOO!"

The top of the rumble seat creaked open, and Bill, a black mound, struggled out.

"Oh, oh, oh!" Smiley collapsed gustily.

"Well, it's his funeral," Dick groaned in relief. "We tried to stop him."

Their voices beat past Bill.

"What's the matter with you two dopes?" His words barely reached them. "What's the delay? Where're the lights? It's darn dark."

"Sure," Smiley shouted, leaning toward him, his hands holding down the rattling roadster top. "That's some of your brilliance. You let the battery go dry!"

"Well," Bill cried, ducking back into the rumble, "there's a flash in here."

The hissing of bushes was a constant, growing undertone. A small cylinder of cold metal was thrust into Smiley's face. He groped for it, its chill smoothness having a reassuring feel.

"We can't sit here all night." Dick shivered. "Let's get going. Now, we can—"

"Look!" Smiley pointed over Bill's shoulder, his hand vanishing in the darkness. "Here comes a car."

Along their back track a glow of light in the sky, outlining the creaking tree-tops, was moving steadily nearer.

"Who'd be along in this place at this time of night?"

"Maybe Cole's got the police."

Bill heaved himself up, starting to clamber out. "We've got to beat them to Craig's."

"Hold on," Smiley shouted. "Wait till we see who they are. They can't get past; we've got them blocked."

The oncoming car rounded a bend and the light blacked on and off, gleaming between tree trunks. Then the lane straightened and the twin beams, dripping light to earth, crept closer.

The boys could hear the throbbing of the motor as the machine jerked to a stop, its headlights flooding over their roadster, dazzling them.

"Hey, up there!" The cry came faint from the other car.

"I'm going to see what they want." Smiley leaped out. "If it's Cole and he starts anything, come after me."

"I'm coming now," Bill gasped between sneezes, but Dick hauled him back.

Smiley, shoved on by the blast, ran along the rim of light, tightening his grip on the flash sagging in his pocket. He passed the headlights and blinked at the sudden plunge into the background of darkness. The warmth of the motor beat out to him. The machine, mudcaked, dirty, had evidently come a long way. It bore a New York license; it couldn't be Cole's car.

As Smiley came abreast the body of the machine, he caught the cry — "Don't! For God's sake, don't! It's just a young fellow — it's not —" A hand holding a levelled pistol was jerked back.

The man at the wheel leaned out, cap pulled low, motoring coat high about his throat. Someone was sitting, silent, beside him. Another man was in the back.

"Is this the way to Craig's? Jim Craig's?"

Smiley's heart, which had thumped painfully at the sight of the gun, steadied, while suspicion flooded his mind. Thinking swiftly, he decided.

"Did you see the crossroads back there?" he asked, attempting to keep the shivers out of his voice. It was better to act naturally, he thought, and make them think he hadn't seen that menacing gun.

The man nodded, his gloved hands shifting wearily on the wheel. He leaned back, then slumped forward, with a tired groan.

"Drive back there and take the track to the right," Smiley directed, trying to see the occupants of the car. "The lighthouse is two miles. Pass that and the road swings to the left. You can't miss Craig's. It's the only house beyond there."

"Thanks," the driver nodded, slipping into gear. "How'll we get out of here? Anywhere we can turn?" He raised his voice as Smiley had to lean closer.

"There's a clearing back around the bend. You can make the swing there."

The man at the wheel turned to his companion. "Train the flash on the rear, Bob, so I can see where to back."

The door banged as the other man climbed out, holding his hat against the racing wind. He directed the light down the lane and the car backed slowly, following the receding glow.

Smiley, lighted by his bobbing flash, raced for the roadster.

"What was it?" The boy's voices rushed at him.

Their faces, eager in the garish light, questioned him.

"There's something up," he said. "Those men were looking for Craig's. I sent them the long way to give us time to get there first and warn him. Come on, Dick!"

Bill started to clamber out.

"Bill, you stay put this time." Smiley was getting mad. "You've horned in enough. You'd make too much noise anyway." He wasn't sure just why noise would be a handicap, but it seemed in keeping. "Get that through your dome."

He grabbed Craig's sweater, and made sure he had the watch.

Bill's huge bulk crawled into the front seat, more protected from the whistling blasts. "All right," he

Smiley knew that wasn't Cole. "What do you want, Craig?" he demanded again, trying to wrench free.

Lights winked up at the edge of the clearing, four of them, like great fireflies. Now they were spreading out, making for the stationary pool of light which was Smiley's flash.

"Put out that flash!" Craig whipped at him, loosing his hold.

Smiley dove for it, snapped it off.

The dog with horrible gurgling chokes, his fore-paws spread and head low, was weaving from side to side, sucking in great gulps of air.

Craig struggled to his feet. "Stay where you are, Karlak," he shouted, "or I'll loose the dog!"

The rays halted warily.

There was no sound from Dick or Bill and Smiley was desperate. "I can't stay here," he cried, but Craig swung around on him, his face distracted.

"Nothing will happen to those boys," he rapped out. "The men are after my father. He was in the car you sent the other way. He'd have escaped only for you!"

Smiley gasped, vaguely aware of the lights once again creeping toward them, "I didn't know that! I thought—"

Craig's words shot out in a desperate stream, "You've got to warn him. Tell him Karlak's here

— to come alone. The boat's ready. You've got to do it. I can't."

From ahead a shout, "Smiley, they're cutting you off!"

Craig gripped Smiley's arm in a torturing hold. "He's innocent, I tell you! Will you go?"

Smiley, overwhelmed at the blunder he had made, was too confused to object. "I'll go — but —"

Craig shouted toward the advancing beams. "Stay back! I warned you!" Then turning on Smiley, "Get going, kid! Keep in line of the trees. Go back of the house!"

Smiley hesitated, wanting to ask more, but Craig, with a hurried shove, started him on his way.

He plunged into the darkness, gripping the chill flash but not daring to use it. He burned as he thought how he'd blundered. And Craig had shoved him to get him going.

From behind him came the shouted exchanges of threats and warnings. Who were the ones who had attacked! Karlak! Then it wasn't Cole's gang and this was no mere kid's battle. Mystery House was on his left, as, hands outstretched, and groping for each step, he moved cautiously ahead. His already hot face flushed deeper as the thought bit into his mind that he was responsible for all this.

He shook his head angrily. He'd have to snap out of it or he'd be getting into a worse mess. Dick had shouted that they were being cut off. Maybe, though apparently he hadn't been missed, some were waiting for him even now. He rounded the back of the house. The lights from the clearing outlined dimly its dark bulk of gables and chimneys.

The cries sounded clearer as Smiley came out of the protection of the house. He skirted the bushes on the far side of the clearing swiftly, like some sinister shadow in a mystery play. He glanced to the left through the scattered apple trees. The flashlights played over Craig and the hound, at bay, the animal straining to get free. Smiley could see moving figures from his angle, which, he knew, must be invisible to Craig, but there was no sign of Dick or Bill. In spite of Craig's reassurance that nothing would happen to them Smiley was frightened. He began to run. He'd get down and warn Craig's father, then speed back here to see what had happened to them.

Wild-rose bushes, combed by the wind, swayed across his path. He was nearing the lane now, utterly unprotected if any flash should be trained on him. A branch stabbed him in the face, raking his eyes. Blinding stars reeled before him as he sucked in his breath in pain.

Instantly a dark shape loomed vaguely before him. "Not so fast!" Strong arms grabbed him. "Who're—"

Smiley whirled, wrenching free. With a grunt of rage he swung the flash, crashing it down with all his strength on the man's bare head. His grip loosened. He slid down along Smiley's body, with a heavy thud into the thorny bushes.

Smiley wiped his aching, tear-blinded eyes to clear them. Then with a swift glance across the clearing he ran for the lane. His headlong flight was apparently unnoticed in the swiftly approaching climax. The confused cries had become more urgent. Smiley swung for one last look before turning into the lane, then halted in his tracks.

Four men, one of them with a raised gun, were closing in on Craig. Their lights focussed blindingly on the man and dog. Craig slowly unwound the chain from his arm as the steady advance continued.

Smiley realized he couldn't see the gun trained on his dog. "Craig," he yelled, "he's got a gun. He'll shoot your dog!"

But even as Smiley started toward him, Craig gave the command, *"Round 'em up, boy!"* The chain dropped free.

The crack of the shot! The animal jarred in the air as if struck by some terrific blow, then fell.

In Smiley's ears echoed Craig's despairing cry.

CHAPTER VI

BUT INSTANTLY the shouting in the clearing had swung toward Smiley.

"There's someone out there!"

He slid to a stop, with windy darkness at his back.

"Get him!"

At the cry beams raced across the narrow lane with its black fringe of tossing bushes. Darting fingers of light crossed and re-crossed. Smiley whirled, bolting along the rutted track which paralleled the shore, away from Mystery House. He feared every instant that some searching light would lick at his heels. He couldn't see his footing as he blundered on, sliding from the slippery grass between the wagon tracks into muddy pools lying in the ruts. Chill water oozed into his shoes.

As soon as he found that no pursuers were after him he went more slowly, but still warily, suspecting some trap. The wind flung itself on him, shoving him back. He turned sideways, shivering in spite of all his running as the blast knifed through his perspiration-soaked sweater as though through cobweb.

After a few minutes the track branched to the right. Straight ahead and leading downhill was the way to Destruction Reef where they had been this afternoon. On the right the lane ran along the cliff beside the ocean. This led to the lighthouse and it was about here that he would meet the car for which he was looking.

By now it was bitter cold.

Anxious about Dick and Bill he wondered what had happened. Who was Karlak? Who were the others? Strangers, he was sure of that much; big men in overcoats which flapped around their shins, hampering them, and felt hats which they kept clapped on their heads against the tearing wind.

Far below the waves thundered on the beach. The gale swept through the nearby trees roaring continuously, *Who? Whoo?*

Smiley bent his head, hugged his arms against his sides. "Yeah," he thought dismally, "who and what, and why did I make that boner?"

The only way he could figure it out was that Craig had been waiting for his father, that the attackers were either enemies of the father's or from the police (somehow he didn't believe that), strangers to this countryside, and that Cole, from the village, had come along as guide.

The heavy scent of lilac, fresh washed by the rain, swept by him, belonging to slow, sunny days, having no strength against a night like this, dark and tempestuous.

He began to worry about the car. "It ought to be here by now," he thought, just as a gleam appeared in the sky, moving slowly behind the lashing, sawtoothed tops of the firs. "That must be them!" Smiley ran toward the car.

The lane straightened. The beams of the headlights crawled toward him, lighting the rutted track, showing up the grass and bushes spread low beneath the onslaught of the storm. Then they blazed over Smiley, planted in the center of the track. He was waving his arms, and yelling even though he couldn't be heard ten feet away.

The mud-spattered machine lurched to a stop, with its motor still running, and Smiley went around to the side.

The man at the wheel, muffled to the ears, cried angrily, "This is the same kid who sent us back!"

"What's up now?" His friend leaned over suspiciously. "What *is* this?"

But the man in the back spoke, silencing them. "What's the matter, boy?"

Smiley shouted his story, sensing the dismay it caused. Immediately the man in the rear seat leaped out. He stood there beside Smiley, tall, broad-shouldered, middle-aged in the eerie glow of the headlights.

"Get back to the city," he ordered the two who had come with him. Behind his words pressed the urgent need of haste. "They don't know for sure that I'm here. They won't have told the police."

"'They,'" Smiley thought, "must be the attackers." Clearly they were not the police.

"Try to locate Spencer." The man's words battled with the gale. "He's my only chance."

"But what'll you do?"

"Get the boat Jim has waiting for me. Go over to the island."

"How can you, Sheldon?" Their voices were incredulous. "Not in this storm."

The blast howled with increasing fury as if it had been belittled. A large bush, wrenched from its sturdy roots, whirled over and over down the lane. From the foot of the cliff came the constant thunder of the waves.

The driver shouted, "No boat can live in a sea like that, Mr. Sheldon. You'd better come back. We can —"

Sheldon shook his head. "I know that boat." He leaned in and spoke a few hurried words to them. "I'll be there before the storm breaks." He lifted a heavy bag over the side of the car. "Watch out for yourselves. So long, boys."

Quickly he turned to Smiley. "All right, what's your name?"

tied the dory. When it was free he tossed the painter into the boat and righted her, the oars rattling across the bottom. He set his bag on the stern seat.

"I'll help you shove her down," Smiley offered.

He picked up the flash. With it in one hand to show the way he grasped the gunwale with the other.

Their legs dug into the sand in short, crunching steps as they strained to start her moving. Her keel grated across small rocks.

Following the path of the bobbing flash they shoved her through pools left by the receding tide; shoved her across swiftly running channels. Wind beat around them. From the dark on either side of the cove came the creaking and groaning of tortured trees. The noise of the surf even in this sheltered place was tremendous.

Now Smiley could make out the water which swirled around mussel-encrusted rocks. From farther out white capped waves boomed, then rushed foaming and hissing up the beach. The motor boat was a vague blur, pitching at her mooring. She wasn't far out from shore and was near the entrance to the cove.

Smiley was appalled by what seemed a piece of madness. "Do you think you can make it?" he ventured.

Sheldon nodded. "Snap out the light now. I think I can. If I don't—"

Foam spread around the prow of the dinghy. Sheldon dropped the locks rattling into their holes, then shot a quick glance at the waves.

"When I get out to the motor boat I'll let the dinghy go. The wind will bring her right back in. Then will you peg her down? She's a good little boat and I wouldn't want Jim to lose her."

"Aren't you going to take the dinghy?" This seemed the crowning bit of folly.

"No. I won't need her where I'm going. She'd only be a drag. Tell Jim I've gone."

A chill crept over Smiley. What was Sheldon's meaning, "I'll not need her where I'm going?"

Craig's father had shoved one pair of oars into the locks. Then, pushing the dinghy free, he leaped in. Before he could pull on the oars the boat was swung broadside, grating against the beach.

Sheldon headed her into the waves again. Smiley shoved her off. The oars creaked as Sheldon dug in with swift, choppy strokes. He was drawing off shore steadily, but the dory was making pitifully slow going. Then suddenly, she rose awkwardly, tilted to one side.

Smiley gave a gasp of dismay. The dinghy was evidently caught on a rock.

But Sheldon, backing water, freed her. Immediately she was swept back on shore.

Sheldon kept her nose into the waves

Smiley waded out. "I'll help you row her to the motor boat. The wind'll bring me right back in."

"Can you swim?" Sheldon demanded.

"Sure."

Laying the flash on the bottom of the tossing dory in case of need, Smiley scrambled in. Sheldon kept her nose into the waves until Smiley shot the extra pair of oars through the locks.

"All set."

The dinghy leaped, as they both pulled.

"Take it easy. The rock's near here." Sheldon guided her to the right, then straightened her out again, making for the motor boat. It was hard to control her as she bucked under the onslaught of the waves. The wind assailed them. As they drew slowly out into the cove Smiley realized that he had misjudged the direction of the wind back on shore. He wondered if it would be as easy as he had thought to get back.

He pulled strongly, his feet braced against the seat opposite him. The rhythmic creak of the locks, the beating of spray against the boat, the rolling of the flash from side to side, beat behind his chaotic thoughts. How could Sheldon make it? If the tide were this strong here in the cove, what would it be like outside? Sheldon would be protected at first by Little Dog. But beyond that was a stretch of sea, studded with small islands, inhabited only by gulls. Some were bleak, rising stark from the sea, others densely wooded. To which of them was he going? Or was it to some unknown island far outside? Navigating even the nearby ones presented tremendous difficulties even to one who knew every inch of the water. It would be madness for a pilot who did not, on a night like this. But Sheldon had said that he knew the motor boat. Perhaps too he knew these waters. Smiley realized that there was plenty about this man which was a mystery.

His arms were aching and his back threatened to break in two. He was weary after his wild exertions of the night, and the strength of the waves he was fighting was tremendous.

"Here she is."

Sheldon shipped his oars. The dinghy bumped the larger boat and their hulls scraped. Smiley pulled in his starboard oar and held the dinghy against the plunging motor boat. She was larger than he had thought. Spray beaten portholes told of at least one small cabin forward, an engine room, maybe some kind of galley. How would Sheldon manage her alone?

"All ready?" Sheldon cried. "Hold her steady and I'll make the change."

Smiley grasped the wet deck of the motor boat. The dinghy rose and fell away. When she went up on a crest, Sheldon leaped easily, the shift in his weight scarcely tipping the dory. He knelt on the deck, reaching down for his bag and one pair of oars.

"Thanks, Smiley. Tell Jim I'm all right."

"Good luck!" Smiley felt a lump in his throat as he shoved off, sliding the oar into black water. Craig's father was going to his death, he was sure he hadn't a chance.

He had headed the dinghy toward the shore when Sheldon cried out, "Hurry up! Hurry!" He was pointing toward the beach. "Get out of line with the boat!"

Smiley, still in the lee of the larger boat shot a glance over his shoulder. Lights were racing toward the water. He saw darting figures. Beams were reaching out toward him.

Swiftly he began to pull for the beach. He didn't want to be caught in any shooting. But at the first stroke, his starboard oar jerked as if hit a terrific blow. A splinter gashed his hand. Numbing pain shot along his arm. Automatically his fingers loosened. The oar slid from the lock. It rose on the crest of the oncoming wave. With a wild yell Smiley grabbed for it but the dinghy swung away, wallowing in the trough. He heard Sheldon shouting but couldn't make out his words.

It had happened so swiftly that Smiley couldn't realize his danger. He pulled hard on his remaining oar, trying to head the dory into the waves. But one blade couldn't control her against the power of the wind and tide. She slid past the motor boat.

He heard Sheldon roar, "Catch the rope! The rope!"

Out of the dimness a coil banged against the dinghy. As Smiley grabbed frantically it dropped into the whitecaps. Then he saw that he was being swept farther from shore. With arms that threatened to tear from their sockets he pulled wildly on the one remaining oar, trying to make the point of the cove.

The wind attacked from all sides. A comber swarmed over the bow and the flash banged back and forth in the water. Smiley was being taken, fighting impotently, out to sea. Spray drenched him. The boat was more sluggish now. The waves were higher. They were racing, oncoming hills of water. The dinghy rose nearly on her beam ends. Another wave slipped over her side. She slid sickeningly down a wall of black water. The oar dug at the air. With a desperate shout Smiley saw the dark arm of the cove fade. He was out in the bay, struggling helplessly in a foundering boat. Beyond lay the storm-lashed ocean.

CHAPTER VII

IT COULD be only a matter of minutes now. The dinghy was logy. The bilge kept up a constant, chopping sound. It seemed impossible that she could mount another comber but again the waves lifted her into the whistling, tearing wind. Smiley could see nothing beyond the glistening, surging black water surrounding the boat. He drooped over the oar, fighting to get his breath. He made a sudden grab for the wave-swept gunwale as the dory slid heavily into the trough. Spray drenched him constantly. In a few minutes the sturdy little rowboat must sink and he'd be floundering in the icy sea. How long could he last in that wild smother?

Suddenly he jerked up his head. For one instant he had thought he heard the beat of a motor. Hope surged up in him as he crouched forward, listening. A howling blast drowned any other sound. But there it came again. There was no mistake this time. It was a motor boat. It must be Craig's father.

Smiley clung to the gunwale of the wallowing

dinghy. She struggled sluggishly to the crest of a roller and rose above the seething waters. Smiley saw a finger of yellow pointing over the stormy sea; a searchlight from the motor boat in the cove. The strong beam searched the waves, shifting slowly from side to side.

Smiley yelled, "*Help! Help! This way! This way! Help!*"

As well might a mouse try to drown out a cyclone. His words were whipped back to him. Desperately he dragged on the oar, trying to gauge the strength of the waves on the opposite side, so that he wouldn't roll helplessly in a circle.

The motor boat was coming out of the cove, plunging steadily through the tossing sea. The searchlight swept by him as the dinghy sank into the trough of the sea. He saw the beam touch the top of the waves and he shouted madly at the dread that he would lose when rescue was in sight.

He pulled again, frantically, till the oar bent, trying to work the floundering dinghy into the path of the oncoming motor boat. Three times the searching light nearly touched him. He was being swept out to sea but Sheldon's boat was making better speed. The sound of the motor came stronger now, a steady beat which grew dim or increased with the noise of the wind. Still Smiley pulled, knowing that if the boat passed him he was doomed. The searchlight swung back. Smiley sprang up in the rolling dinghy, yelling, shouting.

The light struck him, then waves came between. He was swept out of the beam. But Sheldon had seen him and the ray played swiftly across the black, heaving water until it caught the sinking dory again.

The dripping prow of the larger boat swung toward the rowboat. Smiley crouched in the wallowing dinghy, now barely afloat, as gradually the distance between the boats lessened. He splashed through the icy water to the bow and hurriedly coiled the soaked painter.

Sheldon's cry, battered by the gale came faint. "Now! Throw the rope! Throw it!"

Smiley hurled the rope across the narrowing black gulf. It slid across the rail and Sheldon grabbed it. He dragged it in but at that instant a great roller flung the dory crashing against the motor boat's hull. Smiley was flung against the deck as the splintered dory sank. Frantically he clung, catlike, to the wet rail, feeling Death reach for him. He wormed himself up, his desperate fingers clutching at Sheldon's helping arm, then, struggling over the rail, he sprawled onto the deck.

The wind, driving icy spray with it, screamed around him. Then he heard Sheldon, who was at the wheel, cry, "Snap out of it! Come on! You're all right, boy!"

Smiley crawled dizzily to his feet and clung to the stern seat. He wanted to thank Sheldon but couldn't find the words. He kept mumbling, "If you—I—" He stumbled across the slippery deck to Craig's father.

Sheldon, his eyes on the spray beaten, lighted instruments before him, swung the wheel swiftly. "Get below, Adams. There's a bunk in the cabin. You'll feel better in a few minutes."

Smiley's head was clearing. The rolling of the motor boat wasn't as sickening as that of the dinghy. "I'm O. K.," he protested, staring around him. There was no sight of land or anything but stormy water bearing down on them.

Sheldon's face, all lights and shadows in the faint glow from the instruments, turned to Smiley. "Get below, Adams," he repeated determinedly. "You'll have to come with me. I couldn't anchor to land you anywhere. I had to chop the hawser to get to you in time."

Smiley's chill hands gripped the rail more tightly at Sheldon's words.

More than ever now he didn't want to go below. In a sea such as lay ahead of them he didn't want to be cooped up in a cabin, not knowing at what instant tons of water would come pouring down on him. "Isn't there anything I can do here?" he asked swiftly. "Want me to put out the port and starboard lanterns?"

"No." Sheldon's grim expression relaxed a bit. "I guess the fish won't care which side of us comes toward them first. Go get some sleep. I'll call you when I want you. We're in no danger yet."

Smiley's searching eyes saw that there was no fear in Sheldon's face, and also that Craig's father meant what he said. He edged his way down the three steps leading into the tiny engine room. The rhythmic noise was deafening in the enclosed space. He stepped over the high sill into the small, dimly lit cabin beyond. Two short, narrow bunks lined either side of the wall, tapering to nothing at the very bow of the boat.

Black water swirled across the portholes as the laboring boat dug her nose into the sea. Smiley, peering out, caught the gleam of the searchlight lighting the turbulent waves in a weird succession of camera angles. Water swirled constantly across the deck above his head. He climbed to one of the high bunks, pulling the folded blanket around him. The bunk was too short for him so he bent his legs, bracing his feet against the curving bow of the boat. He felt the chill attack of the sea crashing against the stout planking. His head banged against the partition of the engine room as the motor boat climbed a roller. Smiley cushioned it with his soaked windbreaker, then, with a weary grunt, lay still. He thought, "Can we make it?" then of the boys and what they'd tell his mother. Would he reach the island? Sheldon was setting out on a raging sea. The throbbing of the engine beat through his brain. He fell into exhausted sleep, too tired to care.

GRADUALLY Smiley became conscious of a painful grip on his shoulder. He was being jerked back and forth. He caught fragments of Sheldon's shouted words. "Come on! You've got to come on deck! Get a slicker—the locker under the bunk. Come on!"

Smiley struggled to sit up.

As soon as Sheldon saw that the boy was awake he left him. His oilskins brushed against the narrow doorway as he charged through the engine room. Smiley heard the swift thud of his feet mounting the ladder. The tossing seemed to be more violent. Smiley, half-sick, trying to cling to sleep, swung his legs over the raised edge of the bunk. He moved his head gingerly, striving to clear it. The stuffy air, the mingled odor of wet wool from his sweater and the smell of oil made his stomach feel uncertain. Gradually realization came back to him. What was Sheldon calling him for? With a groan he lurched to his feet, teetering there in the narrow aisle. He raised the creaking top of the bunk. It sawed back and forth as he swayed dizzily to the pitching of the boat. He dragged out a yellow slicker, which crackled stiffly as he slid it over his hopelessly wrinkled clothes.

He started for the deck, clinging to the partition to steady himself. The hot engine was still beating steadily. The air reeked of its fumes. Smiley's head came through the open hatch and he crawled on deck. Immediately he saw that the gale had increased. Sheldon was at the wheel, easing it to port or starboard. His face was a grim mask of concentration as he stared at the glowing, glass-enclosed compass. The wind whipped through his oilskins.

Smiley worked his way across the few feet of glistening deck to his side.

Sheldon glanced at him. "You all right?" he shouted.

Smiley nodded. His head was clearing rapidly. His eyes questioned Sheldon's face, trying to see whether the situation were better or worse.

"You can work the searchlight now," Sheldon ordered, leaning toward him. "Keep her swinging as far as she'll go, from port to starboard. If we're on our course we'll pass a bell buoy off to starboard. If we can pick it up we have a chance."

Smiley grasped the wet, icy handle of the light. He swung the beam over the raging sea. They were protected against it by the bulwark in front of them, the raised deck of the engine room.

The boat plunged doggedly into the sea. As the minutes went on Sheldon appeared more worried. He kept urging Smiley to sweep the beam as far as she would go. His eyes shifted constantly from the instruments to the heaving sea.

Suddenly Smiley cried, "I hear something!"

Sheldon reached over, slamming the small door to the engine room, cutting off the throbbing of the motor. Through the noise of the whistling wind and the waves came another sound. A steady, hurried, clang-clang, clang-clang. It came from off to starboard and it was close by.

"Thank God," Sheldon cried. His fingers relaxed for an instant their desperate clutch on the bucking wheel, then he bent toward Smiley. He seemed hesitating as to what he should say, how to say it. "We're in for it now," he cried. "So far we've been pretty well in sheltered water. But now we have to go through a short open stretch. If we're going down it'll be here!"

"Are we near the island?" Smiley shouted.

"Yes, we're headed directly for it. But we've got to run this stretch of open sea. There's no way I can avoid it."

Smiley stared at the heaving waste of water.

A minute later Sheldon slid the catch on the engine room door. "We're going into it now. Watch out. Keep hold of the rail!"

Almost on the heels of his warning the tempest struck full force. The wind raced down on them with breath-taking speed; the waves rose with increased fury.

Smiley gasped, unprepared for the strength of the blast. He clung to the rail and the light, his head lowered against the gale, his feet spread wide on the lurching deck.

The boat shivered, hesitated, then plunged into the violent, lighted sea. The waves thundering down on them seemed mountain high. The searchlight couldn't reach their tops. There was no sound of the engine but Smiley could feel its throbbing through the wet planking underfoot.

Sheldon crouched over the wheel, swinging it hand over hand, pressing his body against it. He favored the boat, taking advantage of every momentary lull to ease the terrific strain. He leaned forward as if by his own strength he could drive her ahead.

"Hold on!" he cried suddenly. "The next one's coming aboard!"

A mighty roller was bearing down on them. They crouched, preparing to meet her. The bow cut into the wave. It curled over, foaming, seeming to hang high above their heads. Then the column of water crashed onto the deck, swirled toward them, curving around the instruments. Darkness. Icy water engulfed them. Smiley was swung against the rail, grabbing it frantically. The boat shook, straining to rise. Water swept across her deck, poured from her scuppers.

Ahead was a wildly tossing sea.

"Get the life preservers," Sheldon ordered, dashing the salt water out of his eyes. "Under the stern seat."

Gasping, Smiley stared at him, then swiftly worked his way along the rail to the stern. He got the rings from the locker, with numbed fingers. He didn't dare think what lay ahead. He fought his way back to Sheldon. Spray deluged them. Waves swept continuously across the deck. How could Sheldon know where they were going? But his eyes never shifted from his instruments except for an instant's glance at the sea. His face was gaunt and lined in the faint, reflected light.

Comber after comber bore down on them. Still the little boat ploughed ahead.

Sheldon sensed Smiley's frightened scrutiny, the mingled hope and fear that possessed him. He shook his head. "The next few minutes should tell. We're very near but this is worse than I thought."

Smiley did the best he could with the flash, keeping the beam moving, trying to pick out the waves which were most threatening. But that was useless. It looked as if each crashing blow must finish her. It seemed impossible that anything built by man could withstand the terrific attack of the furious sea.

At last Sheldon cried, "Keep watch now!"

Minute after minute dragged on. The plunging boat still buffeted the waves. Smiley held his thoughts rigidly to the present, not daring to think what lay ahead, sending the beam across the raging water.

Suddenly he hesitated, swinging the ray as far as possible to the right. "Look!" he yelled, straining forward. "What's that?"

A cliff! Off to the right and parallel to their course.

"It's the island!" Sheldon's voice shook as he swung the wheel to port.

"Did we make it?" Smiley shouted.

Grudgingly the fury of the waves had lessened as they made for the sheltered cove.

"Yes, thank God!"

The ocean hammered against the other side of the cliff. Spray fell like rain over the motor boat as the gale raged in the upper air.

The change left Smiley deafened. It seemed impossible. He grinned weakly at Sheldon. "You were great!" he cried, admiringly.

Sheldon sighed gustily. He opened the door leading to the engine room. The motor was coughing. He and Smiley looked at each other. They had made it only just in time.

The motor boat chugged slowly into the cove. The beam of light lay over water which, though still white-capped, was a mill pond compared to what they'd been through. To the left was a long, low spit of sand, grass covered, pounded by the waves.

"Well," Sheldon decided, "we'll anchor here. There's a fine sandy bottom. We'll have to wade for it, though. There's a dinghy here but she's drawn up on the beach."

With the motor throttled down, they picked up the mooring and Sheldon tied her up securely. He tossed out a sea anchor to make doubly sure.

Smiley took a sounding with one of the oars he lugged from the engine room. The water was shallow, about four feet.

Sheldon was below. His shadow leaped across the rough boards of the engine room as he moved about. When he cut the switch Smiley heard the full fury of the gale from which they had escaped. The motor boat rocked as rough water slapped against her hull. The shifting searchlight played across the deserted, wave-swept beach of the island with its margin of huge black trees. Their tops banged and swayed, testimony to the strength of the storm.

Smiley thought about Dick and Bill. What story could they have told Aunt Jen? His mother? He was sorry for the worry this would cause but there was nothing he could do about it now.

The light in the engine room blacked out. Sheldon came on deck, slammed the door shut behind him, and slid the bolt through the catch. "I'll have to work on the engine tomorrow," he said. Then he looked at Smiley, apparently realizing what all this would mean to the boy. "Jim will be over as soon as the storm eases a little. He can take you off. It's too bad you had to get mixed up in this. Well—" He got a flash lantern from the chest and he snapped it on. "We'll have to get a bit wetter. You take this flash and I'll manage the oars."

Smiley protested. "I'll take the oars. You must be pretty tired."

Sheldon said, "I am."

He turned off the ship's searchlight and pulled a soft cover over it as protection from the salt water. They went to the side of the rocking boat.

"Well," Sheldon spoke. "We'd better get off before the tide comes in. It's about four feet deep now, I guess."

"About that," Smiley agreed. "I took a sounding."

"All right. It's a steady slope up the beach, and you needn't be afraid of holes. There aren't any."

Smiley swung himself over the rail with the aid of the oars. He landed into cold choppy water. "Ow," he roared, "it's icy."

"Hurry up!" Sheldon splashed in after him.

The strength of the waves nearly knocked them off their feet as they staggered toward the shore. Smiley saw that Sheldon was making hard going of it but he didn't know whether or not the older man would resent it if he offered to help him. Before he had decided, they were in shallow water, splashing through the hissing foam. They crunched wearily up the beach. Off to the right raged the gale, with crashing of mighty tree limbs, and the constant thunder of the ocean pounding against the sea barrier.

"How much longer do you think we could have held out if we hadn't made the island?" Smiley questioned.

Sheldon shook his head. "The motor was shot. With that gone we'd have been helpless. It wouldn't have taken many minutes for the finishing touches," he said.

The leaping light of the flash touched the black wall of trees. "The house is this way," Sheldon directed, swinging the light in Smiley's hand toward a thin path. "Let's get there. We'll build a roaring fire and cook a thick steak. Jim's left plenty of

and waded out. The tackle and his sweater he left back on the grass. The waves chopping around his knees were cold, but not chilling, warmed by their long hours of creeping over hot sand.

Smiley grinned. Then he had a sudden conscience-smitten thought of the ones left on the mainland, of Bill and Dick and Aunt Jen. He hoped they hadn't sent word to his mother. But Craig would be over soon, and just now there was nothing to be done. He dismissed his worries and scooped clams out of the mud—four big ones which closed, spitting at him. These he washed off and carried back on shore; with his tackle and clothes he scrambled up the steep bank.

A little farther on, he found an ideal spot for fishing, a low cliff with the waves sweeping against it about five feet below. Smiley settled himself here, braced his back against a tree, and planted his feet in the sandy bank. He baited his hooks; then, tossing the line out as far as he could, waited.

On this side of the island, sheltered from the sweep of the ocean, the kickup from the gale was less noticeable though the glistening water was still far from calm; he wondered how soon Craig would be able to make the trip and in whose boat.

He found a tree trunk which sloped conveniently and leaned against it. The mournful cry of the pee-wee from the woods, the peaceful chirping of other birds, made it hard to believe that on this island was a man hunted for murder, someone unjustly accused who found it impossible to prove his innocence. Smiley wished he could remember more of the case as it had broken in the papers. As he recalled it, Sheldon was a broker, accused of murdering his partner, David Martin or Marlin, at the man's penthouse home in New York. "THE PENTHOUSE MURDER" was the way the scandal sheets had run it. But what could Sheldon prove now that he was a fugitive? What could he do here to substantiate his claim of innocence? Smiley remembered something he had heard last night when Sheldon urged young Larkin and the other man to keep up their search for the fellow named Spencer, that he was their only hope.

There was a sudden twitch on the line and Smiley, roused from his puzzled day-dreaming, leaned over, hauling the line in slowly, hand over hand. When he was sure he had something safely hooked, he crawled cautiously to his feet. A flapping tommy-cod broke from the water.

In the next half hour, he pulled in two more. Deciding that this would be enough, he wrapped them in his sweater and went back to the boat. Sheldon tossed him a frying pan from the little galley, and Smiley went to work.

"That was pretty good," Sheldon complimented,

reaching for his cigarette case when breakfast was over. He snapped it open and offered it.

"No, thanks," Smiley refused, scrubbing the frying pan with sand. "I'm in training just now."

"Yes? For what?" Sheldon questioned with an upward glance, shielding a match in his cupped palm.

"Baseball."

Sheldon blew out the match and broke it. "Baseball, hm? My son, Jim, was quite a star on the Dartmouth team." Pride lay behind his words.

"I know." Smiley nodded.

Sheldon blew a series of slow rings. "Yes, but then this trouble came up and Jim left college to help me. Those two young men who were with me last night are friends of his. The three of them worked out the plan for my escape when it became apparent that every legal means had failed."

Smiley wanted to ask how they had managed an escape from the death house. That seemed such an impossible thing, but he decided he hadn't any right to pry.

Sheldon glanced at him quizzically. "It was quite simple, the way Jim worked it out," he went on, as if reading Smiley's thoughts. "I let them do it only because I knew I was innocent. I thought that, with my freedom, I might be able to get proof. If we can locate Spencer, the elevator boy who has disappeared, I can clear myself. But now—" He frowned, deep in his own thoughts. "The man who is after me, Karlak, is the one, I am certain, who committed the murder. The missing boy's testimony would plunge him into suspicion."

Smiley broke in, "Did Karlak have anything to do with the elevator boy's skipping?" He was well acquainted with the power of the underworld.

"No," Sheldon answered. "The boy was terrified and just disappeared, though they're as anxious to get hold of him as we are but for a different reason." He shook his head, then, as if throwing aside his worries for the time being, went on, "You see, the prison was closely guarded on three sides by high walls." Slowly he traced the plan in the sand with the broken match. "These walls have machine guns mounted on them in case of a sudden break, and also have watch towers stationed at short intervals. In them are guards with tear guns.

"But the fourth side is protected only by Barren River. No other protection seemed necessary because the water, close to shore, is very treacherous and no convict who has ever tried to escape by this route has succeeded. It takes a tremendously powerful swimmer to get through. Canoes and small pleasure boats passing down the safe channel of the river are sometimes beaten by the wind too far in and are overturned. Of course those in them are in immediate danger of drowning. If the convicts are in the recreation yard which fronts on the river, when one of these accidents occurs, always one or two of them who can swim beg the guards to let them go out to help. The guards permit them, of course keeping their guns trained on them constantly. Jim knew this, and on it and the fact that I am a very strong swimmer, based his plan."

Smiley hitched closer, studying the lines Sheldon had drawn in the sand, as the man stared unseeingly at the dying fire.

"On the day chosen for my attempt," he went on, "I was walking in the prison yard with my guard, after the convicts had gone back to their work. Suddenly from upriver there appeared a canoe, the man in her apparently in difficulty. As he came abreast of the prison, just beyond the treacherous water, about here," Sheldon pointed, "he seemed to lose control completely. The canoe overturned and he was flung into the river, crying for help. I ran to the water, my guard after me. As I reached it, he yelled for me to stop, and grabbed me, but I broke free and plunged in, swimming as long as I could under water.

"When I came up, I heard him shouting that if I didn't come back he'd shoot, and in a minute I heard the spat of bullets in the water near me. I dove again, swimming harder than I had in my life. I had to, because the current was threatening every instant to pull me down ; the force of it was terrific, but I managed to come up on the other side of the canoe. At this minute, from the rear came a motor boat plowing along at full speed. She slowed as she came alongside us, and we scrambled aboard. It was as simple as that. There were shots fired at me but the guards were hampered by the fear that the man in the canoe and the one in the boat might be perfectly innocent, people having no connection whatever with me. Though they started after us immediately, we were already down the river and had changed to the car before pursuit was well organized."

Smiley gave a long whistle. It was hard to connect this fantastic story with the serenity of the spring day.

"But why is this man Karlak after you?"

Sheldon ground out his cigarette, and looked at Smiley grimly. "Can't you fill that out for yourself? Karlak is most certainly the murderer. He knows I have escaped and approximately where I am, but he doesn't tell the authorities. Why? If he comes here to the island with those men of his, what will be the result when he knows there's some possibility of his guilt being discovered?"

Smiley guessed he could fill it in for himself. Karlak would kill Sheldon.

"You see," Sheldon said slowly, smoothing the lines in the sand, "my partner, David Marlin, and myself, were the heads of this brokerage firm. Karlak was connected with a bucket shop and I'm convinced that Marlin had dealings with them that were concealed from me. On the night of the murder, I—"

Sheldon stopped, listening, then got to his feet. "There's a boat coming. It must be Jim."

"No," Smiley cried, "that's a plane!"

Sheldon swung around on him. "Get under cover," he said quickly. He kicked the dying embers of the fire apart, scuffed sand over them, and raced for the woods after Smiley.

They stood in the shelter of the trees, peering up. The drone in the sky grew stronger. It was definitely a plane. Then they saw it, flying low.

"It's a Loening Amphibian," Smiley cried, squinting up.

The noise of the motors filled the sky. The ship was directly overhead now; its huge shadow crawled over them. Wind screamed through its struts as it dove directly for the island. Then it straightened out, barely clearing the trees. They could see someone at the cabin window, peering down and pointing excitedly, but not toward them—farther along the island, near the cove where they had landed last night.

"Thank God I hid the boat," Sheldon cried. "They never spotted her."

"But they've seen something else," Smiley cried. "Look!"

The plane was circling round and round a spot which must be either the cove itself or near it. But the pilot was making no attempt to land.

"They *do* see something," Sheldon whispered hoarsely. "Maybe a slick of oil, but I thought I made sure there was none. Watch and see if they're coming down."

"I don't think they can," Smiley objected. "I've built the model of this ship. He couldn't land it on such rough water or he'd never get up again. The strip of beach is too narrow for a runway."

Suddenly the plane climbed, banked sharply and straightened out, flying swiftly back in the direction from which it had appeared.

"Come on!" Sheldon led the way, plunging headlong through the woods to the path. Frightened birds flew up, screaming, at their crashing passage.

They reached the cove, but it seemed just as before. It was full high tide. The glistening choppy water was deserted and there was no path of oil from the motor boat which might have betrayed them to those in the air.

"But they saw something," Sheldon repeated.

"We have to find out what. You search this side of the cove." He gestured towards the sandy bar. "I'll go along this breakwater."

Smiley raced across the hard packed sand and out onto the narrow strip stretching into the rough water. On either side was waving sea grass, nearly covered by the tide with only the tops above water. But Smiley saw nothing which could account for the constant circling of the plane. The sun was hot on his back; he began to sweat and slow down. Sheldon was searching swiftly on the other side of the cove. But he, too, had apparently found nothing.

Smiley began to think they must have been mistaken. In the woods, the birds had begun singing again. The woodpecker was back at his unhurried tapping. There was nothing here, and he was almost at the tip of the bar.

In mid-stride, he stopped, and his heart leaped into his throat. "Mr. Sheldon," he gasped hoarsely. "Mr. Sheldon! *Mr. Sheldon!*" he cried, pointing into the green waves licking the sand.

There in the moving sea grass, floating face downward, moving with the motion of the tide, was the body of a drowned man.

CHAPTER IX

HORROR stricken, Smiley and Sheldon waded out through the clinging eel grass. As they lifted the man's body, water poured from his soaked clothes. Swiftly they carried him ashore, splashing back through water knee-deep, and laid him down.

Sheldon raised a shocked face. "This man's been in the water at least three days," he declared. "Any idea who he is? From his clothes he might be a sailor."

Smiley shook his head, aghast. "I don't know. But maybe he has some papers on him?"

From an inner pocket of the drowned man's jacket Sheldon drew a mass of sodden letters which he read through quickly. "He's Aarne Jansen, 26, able seaman on the schooner, *Nellie Saunders*."

"The *Nellie Saunders*," Smiley echoed hoarsely. "Why, that's the ship which was wrecked on Destruction Reef in the gale a couple of days ago. This must be the man who was lost."

Sheldon got to his feet, sand clinging to the knees of his trousers. His eyes searched the rolling sea.

"The men in the plane saw him," he said slowly and a look of bitterness swept across his face. "And now they'll come back!"

Smiley stared at him, marvelling. Sheldon made no wild recriminations against the fate which had blasted his hopes by bringing the body of the drowned sailor to just this island. There was no railing or complaining. But neither was there any cowardly acceptance of defeat.

"Well," Sheldon said harshly, rousing himself, "the least we can do is bury this boy."

"But," Smiley objected, "they probably think he's you. If we leave his body here when they come back they'll discover it isn't you and most likely go away."

"No. Though if the body is gone they may think that the tide carried it out, still they'll have asked the natives about this place. Some of the old-timers will remember that it was old Tom Larkin's island and Karlak isn't going to forget that Larkin was the name of the young fellow who testified at my trial." Sheldon shook his head. "Too much coincidence. They'll come here and search every inch of ground." He folded the sailor's papers and placed them in his wallet. "Come on."

They crunched slowly back to shore with their burden and there took a breathing spell. The scent of the pines, hot in the sun, was strong. Cheeping sandpipers hurried along the water's edge, their feet leaving delicate tracks in the wet sand. After a minute Sheldon rose and they started toward the woods. A rabbit which had been watching them hopped slowly away.

They had to go more carefully now, feeling for their footsteps over the wet leaves, shuffling slowly ahead. The constant quiet noises of the woods were all around them. Sheldon said shortly, "There's no telling when they may come, Adams; I only hope Jim gets here first." He glanced over his shoulder at Smiley and the boy forced a grin.

"I'm all right," he said. He wasn't frightened by the thought of attack. It was the grim burden they carried so slowly. The finding of the drowned sailor had shaken him more than he wanted to admit. It reminded him of what might have happened last night. He hoped Dick and Bill hadn't sent word to his mother. He knew she'd worry herself sick.

"Go up to the house and get a spade and shovel, will you?" Sheldon's voice cut into his thoughts. "You'll find them in the tool shed right beside the kitchen." He halted, staring across the open, grassy space off from the trail. "This place will do."

"All right," Smiley agreed, straightening up. He ran through the thin line of trees into the sunlit meadow. The red and yellow Devil's Paint Brush made it as gaily colored as a child's picture book.

The wind swayed the flowers until the whole pasture seemed to move.

But Smiley noticed none of it as he swished through the thick grass which laced around his legs. In the shed beside the house he found the tools, rusty but still serviceable, and, after wiping them off on a burlap sack, went back to where Sheldon was waiting.

They worked swiftly, turning over the rich moist earth, not knowing when the first faint beat of a motor boat would come over the water.

"If Jim gets here first," Sheldon's shovel clinked against a rock, "he can take you right off."

"But how about you?" Smiley straightened up. "Aren't you coming?"

"No." Sheldon was brusque. "Naturally I want to save my skin if possible, but that wouldn't be the best way to do it. Jim's boat might be stopped. I'd be found and that would be the finish. Here on the island I have a chance. But," he went on determinedly, "if he doesn't get here first I want you to keep out of the fight. I can make a stand alone, but I don't want to be bothered by you."

Smiley thought, wrenching his mind from their gruesome work, "I wouldn't be a bother, I'd be a help." But aloud he said, "How would this be—? They'll come by boat and probably anchor where we did last night. Then they'll search up to the house. Why can't we go down through the secret passage and then cut through the woods to where they've landed? Most likely they'll only leave one man on guard at the boat. We can surprise him and get away in her."

Sheldon, tossing another shovelful of dirt onto the grass, looked up at him. "Perhaps," he conceded, straightening. "All right! I guess this will be deep enough." He climbed out of the hole.

For a few minutes there was no sound but the shovelling of raw earth back into the grave, then the whacking of the spade to tamp down the sod.

Silently they picked up the tools and shouldered them. "We'll go up to the house now," Sheldon decided after a last look back at the cove. "We can keep better watch from there."

Smiley walked after him, trying to shake off the feeling of depression which possessed him. The drowning of a young sailor, while tragic, was no new story. Each boy who followed the sea ran that danger.

Sheldon seemed to know how Smiley felt for he said, glancing at him, "We'll look at that passage. There may be something to that plan of yours."

"H'mph," Smiley thought, "yes, give the baby a shiny toy and he'll forget his tears."

Sheldon locked the huge front door after them, then inspected the boarded windows which fronted on the ocean. At these unhurried precautions,

Smiley felt for the first time the reality of the expected attack.

"That's about all we can do now," Sheldon decided finally. "We'll make a quick try at that passage, just to make sure that it hasn't caved in if we really have to use it. You know," he explained, as they went along the hall, "we'll be the only ones to go through this place besides old Tom who built it. When he was alive it was sacred and, after his death, when they came back here to settle things they didn't have time to go through it. Besides I guess they wanted to respect his wishes. He never let anyone go through it—always said it meant death."

"Phew," Smiley whistled uneasily. "But he was crazy, wasn't he?" he asked quickly.

"Quite, on that subject." Sheldon stopped before a bolted door near the back of the house. "He always declared that his enemy was after him, some old pirate from the China seas. We used to joke about his enemy, the man with the glass eye, in the summer when we were here—the rest of the year the old man lived alone—" He slid the bar back and shoved against the door. It creaked open protestingly then, jerkily, swung all the way. Smiley trod on Sheldon's heels as he stepped inside.

They were in what was evidently old Tom's work room, a small, comfortable den lighted by a row of portholes, no windows. Beneath them was a scarred bench with neat boxes of wood and tools which the old man probably used in building his array of ship models. One, a river schooner, was almost finished. A beam of sunlight, heavy with dust particles, shone through the drooping, stained sail.

"The entrance to the passage should be about here." Sheldon walked across the little room. "I press the middle knot." His fingers felt over the rough board. There was a click, as of some weight falling into place, and when Sheldon pressed the seemingly solid wall to his right it turned inward, revealing a black hole lying beyond.

"Say," Smiley breathed, trying to go in.

"Hold on. Get something to wedge this door with." Sheldon hooked the box lantern they had used at night to his belt and, flashing it on, leaned forward, his hands on either side of the passage opening, as he stared down. Smiley, a small hammer in his hand to use as a doorstop, pressed close behind him.

Air, chill as that of a tomb, and reeking of decay, engulfed them.

The flash revealed the beginning of a narrow tunnel, braced with beams, some of them already fallen, others sagging. Leading down into the passage were rough, uneven pieces of wood laid on the sloping earth to form steps.

"Good Lord!" Sheldon ejaculated, "that smell is terrible. And look at this!"

The body of a huge rat, stiff and ugly in death, was stretched across the foot of the steps.

Sheldon grimaced as he edged down the sloping entrance. "Wonder if the old boy left it there as a warning?"

"Maybe it's for his enemy," Smiley offered. "Some symbolism meaning that old Glass Eye is a rat."

Sheldon grunted. They both stood there facing into the narrow black mouth lying ahead of them. Smiley looked at the other man, wondering if Sheldon felt the same thing he did—that a spirit of something evil and malignant dwelt in this place.

"Well, come on. Watch out for those rafters; they're none too strong." The bobbing light of the flash led the way, the pitch darkness falling back grudgingly before it. It glittered on rocks jutting from the walls, glistened on slimy tracks running to the floor, where water had seeped through. The tunnel was so narrow that their arms constantly brushed both sides and they had to squeeze by the rotting beams which braced the low ceiling.

The chill, bad-smelling air was sickening. Smiley didn't want to draw a full breath.

Sheldon, a huge black hulk striding ahead, called

back, "Watch out here. These beams don't look any too safe." And, as an afterthought, "There's no telling what the old fellow had in that head of his."

Candle drippings were everywhere. Ends, great blobs of dirty grease, were stuck to the beams. Underfoot were loose pipes, long, thin, which lay in an irregular line along one wall.

Suddenly Sheldon halted. "This is a sell!" he cried. "The tunnel ends here." He swept the light over a jumbled mass of fallen beams and dirt which stretched to the ceiling, blocking their way.

But Smiley had found an opening at the side. He disappeared into it, scrambling over a broken brace of wood. "We can get through," he shouted back in muffled tones, "it's clear here." Then his voice rose sharply, "There's something here! A paper!"

Grunting, Sheldon followed, squeezing his larger bulk with difficulty around the sagging timbers. The light of the flash shone eerily over a board flooring, stained and tracked, and more boards boxed the walls for a few feet. But what had caused Smiley's cry was a streaked paper, tacked up with a long nail. A rusty stain ran from it onto the fine, stiff printing.

In the yellow glow of the lantern they read:

DO NOT ENTER HERE
DEATH LIES AHEAD

"Sa-ay!" A shiver ran over Smiley as he stared into the silent darkness ahead. But the tunnel looked as it had before, the wooden planking of floor and wall had given place again to earth. Tottering beams still braced it. "Let's see what he means," he cried.

"No." Sheldon was impatient. "We'll have to go back. There's no telling when those men will come and we don't know what crazy thing the old fellow has rigged up here. Look at this." He touched a rusty lever extending up from the floor like a gear handle from the bare floorboard of an automobile.

Smiley turned back reluctantly, though relieved a little. "What is it?" He grasped the chill, rust-coated bar and drew it gingerly toward him. Nothing happened.

"Better be careful," Sheldon warned. "Come on."

Suddenly from the wall beside them came a creaking and groaning as of old, unoiled machinery starting to move.

They jumped, not knowing what they had started. The flash swept swiftly across the wall.

"Look out!" Smiley roared, grabbing Sheldon out of the way.

From the boards beside him, at about the height of his waist, came a huge sword, moving parallel to the floor. Back and forth it squeaked. A groove had been cut for it in the opposite wall so that its tip slid into that in its swing.

"Look!" Sheldon gasped, shoving the lever upright. "The old devil!"

The blade snapped back into the wall. The creaking of hidden mechanism gradually died out.

"Well!" Smiley drew a shaky breath.

"Well," Sheldon repeated, starting for the house, "lucky for us that that thing was out of practise. Even so it could have given a nasty blow. The old fellow probably rigged it up so that if he were pursued by his friend with the glass eye he could shove that lever as he ran past, then wait and watch the fellow behind him cut into two."

"He must have rigged up a system of weights," Smiley said. "When it was working right that blade'd cut through the air like a knife."

They followed the jolting beam back to the entrance of the passage.

"We'll only try this tunnel if everything else fails," Sheldon decided. "I'd rather be out in the open where I can see what's against me than cooped up in a hole like this, ready to cave in on me, and where an old devil's been thinking up poisonous plans for his enemy."

Smiley, in spite of his fright, would have liked to see if there were anything else and said so. But

Sheldon answered, "Probably that's all. That's what he meant by 'Death lies ahead.'"

Smiley kept watching to see if he had missed anything. He noticed, now, numerous holes at floor level around the bracing beams, with little mounds of dirt beside them as if some earth animals had burrows there.

The sliver of sunlight from the room above was cheering.

"Terrific odor down here," Sheldon said disgustedly, kicking aside the body of the rat. He mounted the insecure steps and shoved the tunnel door wide.

Smiley picked up the hammer and tossed it into the box of tools while Sheldon unfastened the lantern from his belt and laid it down.

"We'd better see now if there's any sign of Jim or the others, then we can get something substantial to eat." Evidently Sheldon had not found the fish completely satisfying.

The sunlit house, as they mounted through it, was a relief after the darkness and miasmal air of the tunnel. More from a sense of precaution rather than because of any real expectation of attack so soon, they went to the cupola and while Sheldon held the frail ladder Smiley ran up.

He stepped gingerly onto the dusty landing and, scarcely trusting the doubtful looking floor, creaked over to the windows. He rubbed a clean spot on the streaked pane and peered out. The excited chirping of disturbed swallows echoed from the chimney beside him and the muffled beat of their wings was as loud as a blast of wind. Smiley searched the open sea. On the ocean side it stretched deserted, shimmering and glittering in the sun. Then he looked at the cove on the other side of the island.

Instantly he shouted, his face jammed against the glass, "There's a boat moored. It's empty. I can't see anyone!"

"Come down!" Sheldon yelled.

Smiley slid down the ladder, missing his footing and landing with a thump on the floor below. Sheldon was already rushing for the lower part of the house. How long had the boat been there? Who had come in her? Their feet thundered on the stairs. The banisters groaned as they wrenched at them, tearing around the sharp turns. They reached the top of the flight leading into the main hall.

They heard running footsteps on the porch. There was a banging on the barred front door, someone shouting, "Dad! Dad! Are you in there?"

"It's Jim!" Sheldon shot the bolts back and swung the door open.

With a cry Jim Sheldon came at his father. "You made it!" he exulted. "You did it! Gee, Dad!" He stopped, his eyes searching his father's face.

Then he saw Smiley and hailed him, "I'm mighty glad you're safe too. Your friends are worried stiff. They—"

"What'd they tell my aunt?" Smiley interrupted anxiously.

"So far she doesn't know about it. She thinks you're staying down at my place. Dick and Bill have been tearing back and forth all morning, but your aunt thinks it mighty funny, and they won't be able to keep it from her much longer. But I asked them to give me until five o'clock to find out if you'd made it before they spilled the beans."

"You're taking Smiley back with you, Jim," his father cut in. "Right away. When you come again you can bring these parts I need for the boat." He handed him a folded bit of paper.

"Oh, listen Dad," Jim protested, stuffing the paper into his pocket unread, "I want to hear all about what happened. I've got to get back, yes, my team is playing its championship game tonight and I've got to be there but I've plenty of time. Karlak and his crowd had a boat but they haven't any idea where you are."

Smiley looked at Sheldon. Then Jim didn't know about the plane or that the attackers would surely come. Sheldon frowned back at him, warning him not to speak but Smiley elected to ignore it.

"Jim," he said quickly, "there was a plane here

circling the island. They saw enough to bring them back." He explained.

"What?" Jim swung on his father. "You can't stay here now," he cried. "You can't hold out against so many."

"I've told you, Jim." His father halted him. "You get this boy away. Go ahead. I won't take any argument. I know what I'm doing. Don't argue," he cried angrily. "Get going!"

Jim turned slowly. "Come on," he ordered Smiley. "I'll take you over." Then to his father, "I've heard from Tom. The elevator boy hasn't been found yet. But I'll get back as soon as I can. We'll think of something."

"Yes," his father agreed. "There's nothing to worry—" Into his words, freezing them on his lips, came the beat of a motor boat, rapidly coming near. The noise came from the direction of the cove where Jim's boat lay.

"Inside!" Sheldon cried. As he slid the bolt home he leaned over and whispered a few hurried words to his son.

Jim nodded and then glanced at Smiley. "You and I'll try the passage, Adams," he said. "Come on."

Smiley looked suspiciously at him. He was going to be parked somewhere, safely out of danger, he knew that well enough. But he went quietly, apparently completely taken in. "How's your dog?" he asked, as he ran beside Jim down the long hall.

"O.K. Karlak only creased him."

Sheldon looked down on them as he ran up the stairs, making for the cupola.

Jim opened the door of old Tom's den, standing aside for Smiley to enter. Smiley walked inside. He wasn't at all surprised when the door was slammed behind him and the bolt rammed home.

"Stay in there, kid," Jim warned, "and keep quiet. If anything happens to Dad and me, you yell and bang on the door. Then they'll think you're our prisoner and will let you off easy."

Smiley heard him run up the stairs after his father. He considered the room. He had no intention of staying quietly here while a desperate fight went on outside. But the portholes were too small for him to climb through. The door was too strong to batter down and if he did come out Jim's father would only have him put in another room. He faced the passage. He'd have to get out that way. He was at the bottom of all Sheldon's troubles and he'd have to do something to help. Just what he could do he didn't know, as he pressed the knothole and the panel slid open for him. There was no sound from the house behind him as he braced the door after him and picking up the flash lantern went cautiously down into the tunnel.

The horrible odor of decay assailed him and again that warning, the presentiment of evil. He hesitated at the foot of the rude steps, sending the beam darting ahead of him along the black way.

The darkness retreated in time with his slow steps. He kept looking behind him nervously, the farther he advanced. He reached the spot where the message was tacked to the wall, crawled past the rotten timbers and stared at it again. It held him. Was the sword blade the only danger or was there yet another trap into which he might fall? *Death lies ahead.* As he hesitated the timbers bracing the ceiling shook, a thin stream of dirt sifted down as the creaking of the bracing beams testified that someone was running on the grass overhead.

Smiley leaped forward. Evidently the attack had come. He had to get going. The silence, now that the cracking of timbers had stopped, was like a tangible thing. There was no sound but his own stealthy footsteps across the uneven, hard-packed dirt. The warning message ran through his brain. What did it mean? He swept the light up and down, travelling over every inch of space ahead. He remembered long ago reading in a book where, in a passage something like this, a pit of snakes had served to keep off intruders. But there could be nothing like that here. Again the beams jarred, one wrenching free and thumping to the tunnel floor. More earth loosened, fell after it. Smiley increased his pace, scrambling around obstructions, hearing more frequently now that ominous creaking overhead. He'd have turned back, frightened by dread of a cave-in which would bury him alive, but he knew he was nearer the end of the tunnel than the entrance from the house. Gasping for breath, dizzy from following the jerky uncertain light, he rounded another bend. Then, with a wild cry of terror he tried to halt himself and plunged against the chill earth wall. His feet slid on a loose pipe and he fell, the flash rolling away from him.

He yelled, scrambling to his feet, grabbing with one motion for the lantern still glowing eerily. Its light fell unwinkingly over a skeleton, partly concealed in torn black wrappings. The ray glinted on a bit of glass in the deep eye socket, a blue glass eye.

Smiley plunged past into the unknown darkness, racing as if demons were after him. He tore a great gash in his sweater as, panting for breath, he staggered across a pile of nail-studded timbers. He thought nothing now of possible traps. Through his mind raced flashes of the horrible deed which must have taken place down here, how long ago? "Boy," he gasped, "so the enemy did come back!"

The light bobbed frantically onward. His one need was to get out in the open as soon as possible. The tunnel was beginning to slope upward. The air seemed fresher. He pounded up a steady rise. He gave a great sigh of relief and his heart steadied as, through a sheltering fringe of bushes, he glimpsed daylight. He wiped the chill sweat from his forehead with a hand that shook. He halted at the opening just as he was going to plunge outside, caution stopping him. He'd better look around a bit first.

Slowly he moved aside the bushes and peered out. Off to the left through a mass of tangled foliage was the hidden stream. The motor boat in which he and Sheldon had come last night was still moored there, deserted. A faint wind moved the leaves. Nothing else seemed alive. There was utter silence, not even a bird's cry. That seemed odd and at another time Smiley would have waited before venturing out. But the horror lying back in the tunnel pressed him on. He glided through the entrance and was about to move toward the cove when a snapping twig just beside him made him leap back.

A man about five feet away was staring at him—a huge man in overcoat and felt hat—the man who had led the attack last night, who had shot Jim's dog—Karlak. In his hand was a gun, now levelled at Smiley.

Like a streak of light Smiley was back in the tunnel. He tried to wedge a beam across to block the entrance but the man was scrambling after him. He shouted, "Stay where you are or I'll shoot!"

The flimsy barricade fell under his attack. Smiley stumbled back in utter darkness toward the house, not daring to snap on the flash. He was shaking with fright, not at the thought of the pursuer, that wasn't so dreadful, but at the overwhelming fear of having to pass again that gruesome black bundle, rat-gnawn and horrible.

Behind him came steady footsteps, slow but always advancing. Smiley crashed into a mass of timbers. His breath came hissing through his teeth as he crawled past. He'd have to dare the flash. Though it would make him a target still he could make better speed. Let Karlak meet up with the skeleton in the dark!

But before he could press the button he slid to a halt. From ahead, barring his way back to the house came an advancing rumble and crash, the fall of timbers, the cascade of falling earth, the thunder as bracing caved in. The deafening crashes were coming nearer. He turned. A shower of dirt fell on him from overhead. Nearby supporting beams sagged. He snapped on the flash, shouting as he ran toward the entrance. The man was nearly on him. "Go back!" Smiley yelled. "Go back!" But the man came on more quickly. He was yelling something the boy couldn't understand. A falling beam crashed to earth just behind the advancing man, between him and the mouth of the tunnel.

Smiley whirled, but the way to the house was blocked by the cave-in, the way to the shore was blocked by the attacker.

Smiley was trapped.

CHAPTER X

THE CLERK in the drug store at Black Hill had been trying vainly for eight minutes to attract Dick's attention. He had turned out all the lights except the dim, fly-specked one above the soda fountain and now he was re-wiping the already polished marble. Finally with a harassed look into the lighted main street filled with natives all streaming toward the high school he ventured, "Excuse me, but will your friend be much longer at the 'phone? I'm the trainer of the baseball team and I have to get to the game. I have to lock up here. I—"

"Oh," Dick exclaimed blankly, stopping his nervous drumming on the counter. "What?" He turned his worried face from the booth, behind whose closed door Bill was repeating anxiously:

"They've left? Did Larkin say how soon he could get here? What's that?" He screwed closer to the instrument. "Does he know he's to stop first at Miss Adams' here at Black Hill, that we have a message for him from Jim Sheldon?"

The little clerk, with a last desperate swipe of his

cloth, began again, "I have to get down to the game. If—"

Dick stood up. "He won't be much longer now," he promised. He glanced worriedly out into the street filled with jostling, laughing people. The raucous honking of horns, the rattle and squeak of farm wagons, the shouted "Whoa there's," then the uncertain backing of huge horses, their masters, red-faced farmers, at their heads, all intermingled with the constant thud of feet hurrying along the narrow board sidewalk.

Far down at the end of the street a glare of arc lights mounting into the night sky located the school baseball field.

Bill stepped out of the booth. He wiped his perspiring face, then glanced swiftly at the loud-ticking clock on the wall. "Larkin and his friend are on their way," he said in a low voice, as he and Dick moved toward the door. "They should make it by about half-past ten."

Outside they stood at the top of the steps, their eyes roving hopefully over the stream of passers-by. Everyone seemed to know everyone else and the burden of their talk to be, "Mighty smart of Mr. Cole to get up this night baseball. Right thotful. Couldn't git away frum the fahm if 'twas daytime." Mr. Cole this—Mr. Cole that. Clearly Mr. Cole was a power to be reckoned with in the affairs of the village.

One shrivelled little farmer called to another just climbing down from a haycart, "Come to see your boy play, Ernest?"

"Eeyeah. How's your new bull?"

"Mighty nice, thanks. Whyn't you and your old lady come over Sunday t'see him?"

"Thanks, maybe will."

Down the long hill leading into the village streamed a line of honking cars with blinding headlights. They swept into the main street, their blaring horns drowning out the screams of the student passengers, who shouted the praises of Casco High and derided the local players.

The Black Hill folks halted and gave back shout for shout, losing nothing in repartee.

"Oh, Lord," Bill groaned. "I can't stand this. Where do you think Smiley is? What do you think's happened?"

"Don't start that again," Dick begged. "I feel as terrible as you. But I think the fact that neither Jim nor Karlak's crowd came back means that at least Smiley is alive. I figure that he and Sheldon made the island, that Jim found them there this morning, but that Karlak and his gang followed and made an attack."

"How could Karlak's crowd have followed Jim?" Bill scoffed. "We saw them ourselves in a boat just off Little Dog a long time after Jim had left. No, that won't hold water," he finished wretchedly.

"Well, we can't do anything more until Larkin gets here. Are you sure he knows this situation looks mighty bad?"

"I left the exact message that Jim told me," Bill declared. "That if he wasn't back by five o'clock, though he was sure he would be, it'd mean something had gone wrong. I was to send word to Larkin to come, and when he got here to give him this letter." Bill tapped his pocket.

"Well, come on. You've got one more letter besides that to deliver. What time did the principal say we'd find the trainer down at the high school?"

"He said about this time, before the game."

Behind them the drug store leaped into darkness. The clerk darted out, locked the door after him, and pattered swiftly down the steps. As he scurried through the now thinning crowd friends hailed him, "Our boys better be good tonight, Gray. That Casco team looks tough."

He nodded and scurried out of sight.

"Gray?" Bill repeated, starting down the stoop. "Isn't that the trainer's name?" He fished a rumpled letter from his pocket and peered at it by the light from a grocery store where the proprietor was hurriedly and sketchily sweeping out. "Les Gray. Say, that shrimp can't run that team!" He looked at Dick swiftly. "Let's get down there!"

Two cars were speeding through the night, heading for Black Hill. In the lead was the mud-caked machine driven by young Tom Larkin, his face haggard, with lines etched deep by the dust. Beside him was his friend, and in the back of the automobile sat plain clothes men, guns ready across their knees. Behind this machine followed the police car crowded with state troopers. Its siren wailed eerily as they sped through a village, claiming immediate right of way, leaving after them a trail of upflung windows and excited cries in the starry night. "What is it? Rum runners? After the runners?"

Larkin shifted wearily as his car jounced into a sink hole, shooting a pool of muddy water into the air. "This means the end for Mr. Sheldon," he said to the man beside him.

His friend nodded wearily, and said once again, "If we could only get proof that he's innocent. What'll they do to him?"

"Nothing. What can you do to a man who's going to the chair? But Jim will get plenty and so will we."

"If we could only get some clue as to where that fellow Spencer is. But he's too well hidden. Probably in some dive in Hell's Kitchen."

"Or Harlem."

The shrieking police siren drowned out his words.

As DICK and Bill neared the brilliantly, though somewhat spottily, lighted field, the *oom-pah, oom-pah* of the local band and the whistling and shouting of the packed stands came louder. The local team had just finished batting practise and was running up the dark steps to the gym; the Casco squad was streaming out onto the diamond, alert, peppy.

Hurriedly the boys shouldered their way through the standees, working toward the gym.

"Listen, Dick," Bill burst out, "Larkin'll have to borrow Miss Adams' boat. I think we should have told her last night just what happened to Smiley."

Dick considered. "I think Jim was justified in asking us to wait a little while," he said. "No one could have got out a searching boat last night or any quicker than Jim did this morning. But something's gone wrong. He'd never have deliberately left his team. I wonder what he said to the principal in his letter?" Dick went on.

Bill shook his head. "Don't know, but Jim is in a tough spot. That bird, Cole, is likely to cause trouble."

As they crowded past a knot of Black Hill rooters they heard one say, "Hev you heard that Craig ain't showed up yet?"

"Eeyeah. Heard tell."

Bill halted, his face angry.

The farmer continued, "Thet carload of men thet went through last night. They ain't come back nuther. Lonny Cole tells they're inspectors down investigating th' wreck fer th' insurance company."

Bill looked at Dick grimly. "I told Cole last night that I'd tear the tongue out of him unless he told that story about Karlak's men."

They mounted the stone steps, dark, the outermost light scarcely touching them.

"If he's told that team anything about Jim," Bill threatened, over the blare of a sudden skirmish by the band, "I'll murder him."

"Listen!" Dick halted. "If you're going in here looking for trouble, don't. Stay out and I'll give Jim's letter to Gray myself. It *does* look funny that Jim isn't here, you can't deny that. And you can't expect those fellows not to talk, especially after that scene you were in with him down here on the field yesterday morning."

Bill flushed. "I'll explain about that," he promised. "Just let them peep about him, that's all."

Dick pushed open the heavy swinging doors and they stepped into the cool, deserted, stone corridor.

Under the light on the notice board was a printed sign, VISITORS' DRESSING ROOM, with the arrow pointing to the left. From below stairs and off to the right came a sound of pandemonium.

"Down here." Bill led the way, breaking into a run. "They're at it!"

The lower corridor was empty, but at the end a light shone from behind a partly closed door. Terrific uproar and shouting filled the air. Two excited students were evidently supposed to be on guard, but now they were half inside the room, adding to the confusion. Leaping figures struggled back and forth.

Dick and Bill raced down the stone flagging and had almost reached their objective when one of the guards heard them, flashed around with wildly startled face and shouted a warning. Instantly the door was slammed shut. The furore died and an unnatural stillness reigned.

"Where can I find the trainer, Gray?" Bill demanded.

"What do you want with him?"

"None of your business," Bill barked truculently.

Dick cut in, "We have a message from your coach."

From the other side of the door burst a roar which vibrated the length of the hall, "Yeah! Craig the *quitter!*"

"Come on, Dick!"

But the two guards leaped in Bill's way. "Oh, no, you don't!" Their hard hands shoved at his chest.

"Oh, yes, I *do!*" With a vicious yank Bill jerked them off balance and flinging them aside burst through the door into the hot, jammed room beyond, Dick at his heels. "Who said that?" he demanded menacingly.

The uncertainty and worry over Smiley had driven him into such a state that any sign of opposition would bring about a violent outburst. *"Who said that?"* he roared.

There were about thirty boys in baseball uniform milling around in the room; two groups of them, one with Cole the center, the other with a cleancut young fellow as leader. Three harassed business managers were trying to bring about peace between the two factions which were glaring at each other.

"Listen," Dick snapped out. "We want to see Gray. He's to run the team tonight."

"Who says so?" Cole shouted, springing toward Dick and Bill, shoving the others out of the way. "I'm captain and I run the team or I don't play!"

The other boy, leading the smaller group, blurted, "The game's on in half an hour. The Casco team's nearly finished their practise. What's the matter with you? The principal said Gray was to run us and now the coach says the same thing."

"That's the stuff!" Bill seconded. "It was absolutely impossible for Jim to be here but you've got to play without him. Gray will handle—"

"*No!*" Cole shouted.

From the small, lighted inner office Gray appeared, standing nervously in the doorway. "What's this?" he cried, with an attempt at authority.

"Aw, go back to bed," Cole roared inelegantly. "You heard everything. Don't pretend you didn't."

"Now, Lonny—" Gray advanced timidly.

"Don't 'Lonny' me, you old buzzard."

Gray halted, his face already a painful red, flushing yet deeper. Bill looked at Dick as Cole kept up his merciless baiting and the little trainer retreated. Cole's crowd, laughing and shouting, urged their leader on, while the other small group and the business managers tried vainly to intervene.

Finally Gray, backed into a corner, cried wildly, "I'm going for the principal! I'll tell Mr. Hotchkiss this outrage is—" He tried desperately to dodge past but Cole bounced in front of him, laughing, at each try.

"No, you don't snitch! You stay right here!" He shoved Gray forcibly down on a bench. "You stay there till we're ready to go out. I'll run the team. I'm captain and it's my right! See?" He swung toward Bill, the fringes of his mob sweeping after him whichever way he turned.

"See what?" Bill asked softly.

Dick, knowing his temper, pressed close. "Take it easy, Bill!"

But Bill paid no attention. "See what?" he repeated. "A dumb bully and clown? Yes. Isn't that what I'm supposed to see?"

"I'll fix you, too," Cole raged, springing toward him.

Bill grinned, his fists clenching slowly.

Cole planted himself in front of Bill, directly before the inner office. He smirked nastily. "I say Craig's a dirty quitter," he repeated, "and I say—"

"Look out!" Bill warned.

"—that he's a rotten coward, afraid that I'll show him up!"

Bill leaped, crashing his huge bulk into Cole, snapping his mouth shut with a click. The force of his charge bore them both, with Cole yelling and clawing, into the inner office. Bill kicked the door shut behind him and, fumbling with the key, turned it in the lock.

Cole's cries, "Help! Help!" came frantically at first, then apparently he realized that help wouldn't come and began to fight.

Help couldn't come because Dick, swinging two

bats, had leaped in front of the locked door with the warning, "If one of you tries to bust in I'll tap him with these!"

Cole's followers shoved and pushed, trying, but not quite daring, to rush Dick. The other group of boys, grinning with delight, spread into line before him.

From the locked room came the crash of overturned furniture, thuds and explosive grunts as blows struck home. Fighting shadows lurched across the glass panel. It was impossible to tell who was winning. Suddenly there came a terrific smash, then the tinkling of glass and a rush of water.

"The water cooler!" one of the boys yelped.

Then from inside, from down on the floor came the cry, *"Will you play? Will you?"*

Muffled grunts.

"Will you?" Crack!

"He's banging Lon's head on the floor! He'll kill him! Rush him! Rush!" yelled one of Cole's followers from the rear row, well out of danger of a tap from Dick's bats.

"Stay back!" Dick warned. "I mean it. Don't try to break in!" Though he wished earnestly that something would stop the fight before one or the other was murdered.

Roars of maddened rage from behind the door. The baffled drumming of heels against the floor.

"I'll play! Lemme up. Get off of me, you big bully!"

Bill's shadow moved across the glass, the key turned and the door was opened. Bill stepped out, breathing heavily, but with dignity, jerking his tie from under his ear, tucking in his shirt.

"He'll play," he announced laconically.

Dick, with a swift glance at him, ran inside.

Cole was crawling to his feet, groaning; one hand clapped over his eye.

Dick took one look at him. "Bill!" he cried.

The players came surging through the door and Bill had to elbow his way back.

"Look at him, Bill. He couldn't play tiddly-winks!"

Bill jerked Cole's arm down. His face lengthened. Cole was a sight. His two eyes were closing rapidly.

At the astonished whistles and gasps of his henchmen, Cole stumbled to a mirror and peered dazedly at himself. He began to blubber.

Bill cried, "Gee, I'm sorry I hurt you so much. I didn't mean to."

Cole wrenched free. "You didn't hurt me!" he snarled. "I fell!"

He heard the low "*Razz-berries*," and whirling on the crowded room bellowed at Bill, "I fell, I tell you! You'll pay for it! I'll have my father fix you. I'll settle you and Craig and Gray and old Hotchkiss. My father'll take their jobs away. He'll—" his voice cracked.

Bill went over to him. "Shut up, kid. You're all wet."

A slow hush had settled over the crowded office. Gradually, row by startled row they turned around, all but Cole who kept up his sobbing threats.

There in the doorway leading from the main corridor was Gray who had slipped out unnoticed. With him were the three befuddled business managers. But the man standing there calmly, the man who caused frantic whispers to race back and forth, was small, white-haired, kindly-looking. The principal of Black Hill Academy, John Hotchkiss.

In frightened silence the boys fell back. Cole stood alone except for Bill and Dick, his hands over his face, his broad shoulders shaking.

"That will be all, Leonard Cole!" The principal's voice was low, but it sent a shiver through the crowd. The boys stood tense. Not a foot shuffled. The muffled *ta-ra-ra, ta-rarara rarah* of the band seeped through the closed windows. "Take off your uniform and go home! Do not return to class!"

A sigh raced across the room.

Cole gave a choking gulp but didn't lift his head. He shuffled slowly out toward his locker, a way opening up for him.

"Old Hotchkiss has got guts," Bill rumbled to Dick. "This may cost him his job."

The principal glanced at Bill, and Bill grinned back at him admiringly.

Mr. Hotchkiss unfolded a creased paper he had been holding. Then slowly, into the dead silence, he read a list of names, all of them belonging to members of Cole's crowd, and all hecklers of Gray. "Those whose names I have read cannot represent the school in the game tonight," he finished quietly. "Turn in your uniforms. The others on the team whom I haven't named will play for Black Hill tonight. That will be all until Monday."

One of the distracted managers, hurriedly counting noses, yelped, "Mr. Hotchkiss, that leaves only seven men, not enough for a team. We have to have at least nine!"

The dismissed members glanced at each other and grinned triumphantly; the old tyrant would have to let them play!

The principal hesitated an instant, his face tightening, then said, "I'd rather call off the game than have the school represented by players who are not good sports. I shall see the Casco authorities and make my apologies to them." The door closed after him, firmly.

To call off the game at this late hour would be a catastrophe. The stands outside were already crowded. The explanations would bring disgrace on the school. Craig would be utterly discredited and blamed for the whole affair.

"Gee," Bill cried desperately, "can't we think of something? If Smiley were—"

Dick gripped his arm. "Listen! I know what we can do! You and I'll play on their team. If the principal's willing and Casco agrees, why not? In an emergency like this they ought to stretch the rules. We—"

"Gray!" Bill shouted to the little man, again the center of a milling group, besieging him with wild questions. "We'll play for Black Hill if your principal and Casco's coach are willing. Want me to find out?"

Gray bleated, "I—I—I don't know—well—oh—"

"*Yes!*" The seven members shouted as one, drowning him out. "*Yes!*"

"All right!" Bill cried. "Where're your managers? They can come with me. Dick, see what sort of line-up you can scramble together."

With the three wildly hopeful managers tearing after him, he crashed through the crowd to the hall.

Immediately Dick, heckled by the dismissed boys, got together the seven remaining players. "What positions do you play?" he demanded.

The boy who was the leader, the cleancut chap called Hinckley, spoke up, "We don't play any."

"What?" Dick cried, aghast. "What d'you mean?"

"We don't play any. We're the subs."

Dick clapped his hand to his head. "*Ohmigosh!*"

"Hinckley was *once* a regular," one declared.

When Bill came rushing back with the information that Mr. Hotchkiss had agreed that they might play and the Casco coach was willing also, and was then checking up their credentials by phone call to Westbury, Dick, with Gray's help, had assembled something resembling a line-up. He and Bill would play second and first base, respectively, their regular positions in the Westbury infield, and would bat third and in cleanup position. Hinckley would pitch.

The news that not one of his team was on the regular squad stumped Bill for only a minute. "That's O.K. We'll beat them by a bigger score than the regulars ever could!" He turned to one of the hovering managers. "Rassle me and Dick uniforms," he urged, scrambling out of his clothes. "We've got to get out there right away!"

Swiftly he cleared the room of all but Gray and the seven players, sending the dismissed men out into the hall. Then the trainer explained to him about the various boys and the positions they were able to play. Hinckley was a pitcher who was either a sensation or terrible. He had been ruined by overwork the season before Craig took charge and his pitching had gone to pieces. Craig had labored with him patiently, giving him every chance, but he always blew up when the going got tough.

When he and Dick were dressed, Bill began, tightening the belt around his lean waist, "Now, fellows, you know what you're up against tonight. You know what you've got to do." Then he gave them a pep talk which the late Knute Rockne had used one time at Notre Dame, changed slightly so as to apply to baseball. But no Notre Dame team had ever needed the talk one tenth as much as this scrambled team of substitutes. To Hinckley, Bill said, drawing him aside, "Jim Craig has the greatest confidence in you. Tonight, you've got to show that he's right. You know that these boys can't give you the right support or they wouldn't be subs, but you can win your own game. You've had plenty of rest and you're ready to go. They say you blow up when it gets tough. Well, blow up to high heaven but do it before you get out to the mound. Your folks are out there?"

"Yes."

"Well, they want to see you win. Don't disappoint them!"

Just as they were ready to go out, and the steady

cheering from the stands came through the windows, one of the managers hustled the mascot up to Bill. This was a small colored boy, about ten years old, whose name was Happy Landings.

Big Bill, standing beside the little fellow, saw a chance for something dramatic.

"Happy!" he cried, bending down. "How much are we going to win by?"

The little fellow opened his mouth, which was about half the size of his face and rimmed by glistening teeth.

"*Yas, suh!*" he shouted.

"Hear that?" Bill cried exultantly, clapping the mascot on the back. "Let's go!"

The boys cheered and sprang to their feet, leaping for the corridor to the field.

"They *look* like ball players," Bill said to Dick as the two of them ran out after the pepped-up squad. "But it's up to us, Dick."

Dick nodded. The first player raced down the gym steps. The roar from the crowd was deafening. It soared up to the lights, making them quiver. "This may make some trouble about our playing on our own team," Dick commented.

"I know," Bill agreed, plunging after the rest of the players, "but they can win without us back home and Craig sure needs us here tonight. Let's beat 'em!"

CHAPTER XI

THINGS happened swiftly in the next few minutes. Bill and Dick were everywhere; conferring with the umpire and the Casco coach, checking over the line-up and getting the players out on the field. Bill, who was acting captain, had Hinckley warming up, and was watching him anxiously. He hated to send the boy into the box after such a short time to limber his arm, but that was only one of the handicaps. So far Hinckley seemed to be doing nicely. He showed control, and Bill, who had been a sensational pitcher before he was converted into a first baseman in order to make use of his terrific slugging, knew just how vital that was.

The night air was chill. In the short intervals when the stands were not clamoring for the game to start, the cry of frogs sounded from the swamps off in the darkness beyond the athletic field.

Bill glanced quickly around the infield, where at the crack of the bats the fielders scrambled for grounders. Some speared them nicely, others overran the ball, but all were trying.

Dick ran over to Bill. "They've got lots of pepper, but they're not so hot, if you get what I mean," he declared, adjusting the padding in his borrowed mitt. "But say, do you realize that we've never played at night before? We may not be such marvels ourselves."

Bill grinned. "Why bring that up? Haven't we enough worries?"

A great cheer swelled through the impatient stands.

"Well, we've got to start now. We'd better wish ourselves lots of horseshoes."

With Bill's exhortations ringing in their ears the Black Hill players trotted out to their places. Hinckley walked firmly to the mound, and Bill told him, encouragingly, "Remember, we're right behind you. Show 'em Craig was right about you."

Swinging their war clubs the first two Casco batters left their dugout. Bill, stationed at first base shot a glance over the field to make certain his men were in at least approximate positions. At second, Dick was pepping up the shortstop. Hinckley was taking slow practise pitches, shooting the ball into the catcher's mitt.

The umpire bent over and dusted the plate with a tiny whiskbroom.

Hands on knees, Bill crouched ready. It ought to be lambs to the slaughter, he thought swiftly, realizing that in addition to everything else Hinckley probably knew very little about the Casco batters, what their peculiarities and weaknesses were. His lips tightened grimly. Well, he'd see what he could do. Then the cheers ringing through the night all died for him; he became utterly oblivious of them at the cry, "*Play ball!*"

Snapping his cap down on his forehead Bill shouted, "Let's go, gang!"

The catcher tossed a new ball out to the mound. Hinckley rubbed it slowly in his hands, his glove pinned under his right arm. The catcher squatted, pounding his mitt hollowly, but this meant little in the way of signals, since he, also, was practically ignorant of the kind of balls to feed the various Casco hitters.

Now the first man was up; a little pint-sized rabbit, a hard fellow to whom to pitch. He crouched over the plate, waving his bat.

The teams were ready. The rooters had been ready for an hour.

Hinckley wound up.

"Ball one!"

A wild cheer from Casco.

"Ball two!"

Hinckley's face was strained; the incessant roar of the crowd seemed to bother him.

"Forget the stands," Dick cried from his post behind the pitcher.

"Ball three!" The umpire's lips moved, but his words were drowned by the howling stands.

Bill shifted uneasily, digging his cleated shoes into the dirt. "That's O.K., Hinckley," he shouted, pounding his fist into his mitt. "Take it easy. You'll settle down." He and Dick started to chatter, talking up a good game of ball, for they saw that the shortstop and third baseman were nervous and upset because Hinckley couldn't find the corners.

Then, "Strike one!"

"That's the way, boy. That's pitching."

"Strike two!"

The stands roared.

Again Hinckley wound up.

Then, crack! A hard hit grounder shot toward Bill, a little over to his right. He darted for it, made a dazzling stop and, while still doubled over, whipped the ball to Dick who had covered first.

Up jerked the umpire's arm. "You're out."

One gone. And now all the boys began to talk it up. The tension had lifted. The most difficult lead-off man in the circuit had gone out in a great play well executed. They were good! They were better than the varsity!

The second Casco man was easy, as Hinckley tightened up like a new shoe, and the third batter went out swinging.

As Black Hill dashed for the dugout Hinckley was the recipient of loud words of praise. "Nice work, Hink. Keep it up." He grinned as he slipped his slim arms into his sweater and, shouldering through the laughing players, worked his way to the water-cooler, tended by the jubilant Happy Landings.

Gray went out to the baseline to coach. The little fellow, bundled in a Black Hill sweater, swelled with importance.

Bill crouched at the front of the dugout, watching every move on the field, sizing Casco up for a peppy, alert outfit, which packed plenty of punch. "Now, fellows," he advised Carter and Jordan, the first men up for Black Hill, "get a homer apiece."

Happy Landings offered them their bats, and, swinging lustily, they moved out into the waves of cheers. Carter stepped into the batter's box, tipped his cap nervously and waited, bat on his shoulder.

The Casco pitcher, Martup, shot the first ball.

"Strike one!"

The frantic cheers of Casco were balanced by the boos from Black Hill.

"Strike two."

Carter fidgeted anxiously, but did not take his bat from his shoulder.

"Strike three, and out!"

"Well," Dick commented, "he did all his swinging before he got to the plate."

Bill shifted his glance out to the diamond where Jordan was duplicating Carter's feat. He was a tall fellow with an awkward stance, something like that of Al Simmons. But his batting was nothing like that of the American League slugger. He went out swiftly on three beautiful strikes.

"Powerful hitter we have. Well, we're up next, Bill." Dick selected the bat he had chosen for his own.

Bill reached for the stick Happy Landings had ready for him. He turned to the men who had just been at the plate. "Say," he barked, "you birds have to take a cut at the ball. Don't go out with your bats on your shoulders. Watch us, now."

He knew the team was upset because they hadn't so much as tipped the ball and he determined to do his best to snap them out of their gloom before it was too late.

Dick was at bat first, so Bill, resting on one knee, studied Martup. The pitcher worked smoothly, with little waste motion, and did not look like one who would be easily rattled.

"Get on, Dick," Bill exhorted.

Dick waited, relaxed but alert.

"Strike one." Dick swung around on his heels as he missed the ball.

"Strike two." Casco shrieked as Dick did not offer at a fast one that just nipped the corner. Bill's eyes narrowed. This bird had a deceptive curve.

"Ball one." Dick refused to bite at a teaser.

And "Ball two."

Once more Martup took his windup.

Crack! Dick connected with a nice single which the third baseman knocked down but could not handle. Dick was resting on first as Bill came to bat, grinning.

Black Hill was frantic. From the main street came the honking of hilarious auto horns.

Dick cupped his hands around his mouth. "Bring me home, big boy," he shouted to Bill, taking a good lead off first.

Bill pointed to right field, his favorite place to drop a homer, then, settling his cap, he tapped the plate and waited, swinging his bat in slow arcs.

The Casco infield was talking it up, urging their pitcher on.

Thud! The ball sank into the catcher's mitt.

"Ball one."

"Ball two."

That hit of Dick's had unsettled Martup for a minute. The catcher walked out to have a talk with him. Dick waited on first, hands on hips.

Martup was ready to pitch.

"Strike one." Bill let that go by.

Crack! Dick connected with a nice single

The catcher, thumping his glove furiously, yelled, "That's getting 'em. This egg's easy."

"Strike two." A blinding fast ball.

Two and two. Bill crouched, eagle-eyed. He had a hunch that the next would be a slow ball. It was.

At the crack of bat and ball Dick started around the bases. The fielders were racing for the ball. It dropped safe and rolled away from them. Dick tore home. Bill thundered around second, Gray, waving and shrieking like a madman, urging him on. The third baseman was waiting for the throw-in, but Bill slid in under him, safe. He jumped to his feet, slapping the mud from his uniform and grinning at the noise, but not bothered by it one way or the other.

Now Allen, the shortstop, was at the plate and Bill took a long lead off third. He darted back and forth, arms swinging, ready to steal if there were the slightest chance of it. But he had no opportunity, for Allen went out on strikes.

Score at the end of the first inning, Black Hill 1. Casco 0.

"Well," Bill said to Hinckley as Black Hill streamed out to their positions for the start of the second inning, "you've got something to work on now, boy."

The result of that score was soon apparent, for

Hinckley settled down like a veteran big leaguer and Casco could not get the ball out of the infield.

But Black Hill did nothing either with the tail end of its line-up. There was no scoring at all until the last half of the third. This didn't start impressively for Carter grounded out, and Jordan flied out. So two were down when Dick stepped to the plate.

He wasted no time, but lashed the first pitch over second for a nice two-bagger.

Now Bill was up, welcomed by the frantic cheers of the stands. The lights shook under the pounding of many feet. Casco held a hurried conference, the catcher and whole infield clustered around Martup. Then the catcher trotted back, settling his mask and grinning through it at Bill.

"Ball one." It was way wide.

"Ball two."

Then Bill knew just what that grin of the catcher's had meant. They were going to walk him deliberately to get at the weak-hitting Allen. Or, they thought they were.

"Ball three."

Bill swung his bat carelessly with one hand, as if he expected to be passed and was getting ready to go down to first. But the instant Martup started his windup Bill tightened, and crouched ready. The pitch was going outside. Instantly Bill stepped into it with a full swing.

There was no doubt where the ball was going; home run was written all over it. Bill made the tour of the bases, bombarded by cheers from hoarse, aching throats. Dick was waiting for him. "Just keep that up and we'll win in a walk."

"It's in the bag," Bill predicted confidently.

So the score was Black Hill 3, Casco a goose egg, at the end of the third inning. And that was still the score going into the last half of the seventh. Hinckley had been pitching a wonderful game, with the players giving him brilliant support.

Bill and Dick were not worrying as they watched Hinckley, the first man at bat, go up to the plate. "Take it easy," Bill advised. "No need of tiring yourself out."

The Black Hill folks applauded their pitcher enthusiastically.

There was no hint of what was to happen.

On his two previous trips to the plate Hinckley had struck out and hit into a triple play, hardly a great record. Now, evidently elated by the applause of the rooters he determined to try for a hit. But Martup, too, had been pitching nice ball, and now he wasn't particularly worried at having to face his rival. He shot in low fast ones for a strike, a ball, and a second strike. Then it happened. Hinckley was hit by a pitched ball.

Instantly, as Hinckley doubled up in pain, grasping his pitching arm, Dick and Bill raced from the dugout. Martup and the Casco infield crowded in. "Awfully sorry that happened!"

Gray came pushing importantly through. "How's it feel?"

"It's all right. It's fine. Forget it." Hinckley straightened, protesting that he would be all right.

Bill grabbed a sweater from Happy Landings and made Hinckley slip into it, as he moved toward first base.

"How does your arm really feel, Hinckley?" he demanded.

"It feels a little numb, but it'll be all right," the pitcher said, reassuringly.

Bill ran back to the dugout. "I don't like this a bit," he declared to Dick. "I got a crack like that one day and my arm went completely dead. I didn't want to start him worrying but we'd better be prepared." He turned to the silent players. "Do any of you fellows pitch?"

None of them did.

Bill picked up two mitts. "It's the bull pen for ours, Dick. We'll see if I still have Mary Ann."

The startled players stared after him, bewildered.

Out on the field Hinckley was taking a nice lead off first base. There was a sudden crack as Carter shot a clean single over second, and Hinckley sped around to third. Bedlam broke out. The fans started pounding their feet on the wooden stands, thinking Martup was about to blow up. But their joy was short-lived, for Jordan hit into a double play, which erased Hinckley as he slid for home. Then Dick came in from the bull pen and was passed. This brought Bill up, but before he could get a chance Jordan, who had got a life through virtue of a fielder's choice, was out stealing.

So the score at the beginning of the eighth was still 3–0 in favor of Black Hill, and so certain were the fans that the game was all over that they started to drift down toward the field barrier. But Bill and Dick watched with anxious eyes.

The first man to face Hinckley was Martup, Casco pitcher. There was apparently nothing to fear from him, but to the wonder of the crowd Hinckley passed him. Bill gritted his teeth. This was the tip-off on Hinckley's condition. He ran over to his pitcher. "Do you think you can hold them?"

Hinckley's face was drawn, under the garish lights. "It'll be all right."

Bill went back to first. Now the head of the batting order was up, the little fellow, hard to pitch to under any circumstances, but doubly so now that Hinckley was in trouble. He made Hinckley bear down, by refusing to bite at a bad ball. Finally he worked a pass, and accompanied by the mounting cries from the stands, flung aside his bat and trotted down to first.

Two on, nobody out.

The catcher ran out to Hinckley for a conference. Then Bill and the whole infield went over. "Can you hold 'em, Hink?"

Sweat stood out on the young pitcher's forehead. He nodded grimly.

Two on, nobody out. Hinckley wound up.

There came the sharp crack of bat against ball. Bill leaped high in the air and came down with a screaming liner. He was ready for a double play but the men had scrambled back to their bases.

Two on, one out. The situation had eased a trifle.

But the next man walked. Three men on. Then began the constant cries, "Take him out!"

Bill turned a raging face to the stands. Couldn't they see that Hinckley was giving everything he had? Bill stared across at Dick. He hated to yank Hinckley when victory was so near, and after he had pitched such a fine game, but it was rapidly being tossed away. Still, if only he could get a double play.

The man at the plate was ready. Hinckley shot a fast one in to him. But there was no deception to it. A hit went screaming over the fielders' heads, rising, rising until it finally cleared the right-field bleachers.

Score Casco 4, Black Hill 3.

The pandemonium in the stands was frantic. Screeching fans bellowed, "*Take him out! Take him out!*" Others shouted, "They haven't anyone else!"

Bill ran out to Hinckley. "O.K., boy," he said. "You've pitched your heart out for them. I'll take it over now."

The players cried, incredulously, "You a pitcher?"

Bill slipped his hand out of his fielder's mitt. "I was. Now, Hinckley, you play first base. Give me your glove."

The players went back to their stations. For the minute the stands were silent, waiting to see what was coming. Bill walked to first with Hinckley. "Don't pay any attention to those clowns in the stands," he told the heart-broken boy. "When you're winning you're great. When you're losing you're a bum. You pitched a grand game and it's a tough break that you couldn't finish it."

Then Bill announced to the umpire that he would pitch for Black Hill. While the umpire was telling this to the crowd Bill cornered the catcher. "Listen," he gritted, "I've got a sinker ball and that's all I have. When it's working right no one can hit it.

They either knock it into the dirt or pop up. Now you've got to be on your toes."

The Casco batters came crowding to the plate. Bill waved at them. "Only two of you'll have the honor of facing me this inning," he predicted, "and neither of them will do anything."

Swiftly he took in the positions of his men, then faced the plate. There were only two innings to go so he could give everything he had. He unleashed a few practise pitches and grinned, for old Mary Ann, his sinker ball, dipped just as she used to. He swung around to Dick. Dick clasped his hands above his head, shaking them enthusiastically.

The batter was in the box. Bill tightened his belt, and scuffed the dirt around to get a satisfactory toehold. He took a quick windup and whipped the ball for the plate.

Crack! The ball bit into the dirt before the plate. The catcher pounced on it and shot it to first ahead of the runner. Two out, nobody on. And the next man went down swinging wildly at a ball he couldn't seem to touch.

"Now," Bill shouted above the frenzied roars of the crowd, "let's get that run right back." But they did not get it right back. In that last half of the eighth, Bill got his base on balls. Allen was also passed, but the next three went out on an infield fly, a strikeout, and, after another pass, a second strikeout.

Score at the beginning of the ninth still showed Casco leading by one run. Bill held Casco scoreless in her half of the ninth and then came Black Hill's last chance.

The head of the batting order was up. This was Carter. After an agonizing delay, when the count went to three and two, he struck out.

Assailed by the deafening roars of Casco, Jordan came to the plate and hit the first ball. It was taken easily by the centerfielder.

The screaming was continuous now.

Two out, none on, one run behind. Now it was up to Dick. If he failed the game was over, lost.

Bill grabbed Dick by the shoulder and shouted above the uproar, "If we get on we'll try it. It's our only chance. When I yell, 'Smiley,' that'll be the signal!"

Dick grinned and nodded. He went up to the plate, swinging his bat confidently.

Deathlike stillness swept over the stands. Dick was passed. Then the tornado of cheering burst out again as Bill came to the plate. But Casco refused to let him hit, and he was passed intentionally, as he had expected.

Now Allen was at the plate. He crouched there in desperation, but Bill and Dick knew that if the game was to be won it was up to them. Bill made sure of his belt.

Martup looked them over carefully, making sure they were not too far off the bags. His first might be a pitchout, but they had to take the chance. They couldn't let Allen gum up the works.

Martup wound up.

"Smiley!" Bill yelled.

Then it began, the scene which reduced those who saw the game to whispering wrecks for the next week.

The ball left Martup's hand. Like darts Dick and Bill tore away. Dick slid into third as the catcher pegged swiftly to that base. Bill was thundering toward second. The third baseman flung the ball to the second baseman as Bill pounded in, safe. The ball went over his head. It was stopped by the shortstop who was backing up. The wild screaming told him something was happening. Dick was streaking toward home. Desperately the shortstop shot the ball to the catcher. Bill left second. Dick slid into home, safe, as Bill was racing for third. With the screams ripping the night the frantic catcher whipped the ball to third. But Bill had already touched the base, rounding it under full steam, and was pounding for home. The ball sped after him. It struck him in the back and rolled free. The yelling catcher dove for it, turned to whip it home. Bill was already there, grinning, the only silent, motionless person in that whole ball park.

Black Hill had won, 5—4.

Like juggernauts the Black Hill players swept from the dugout and hoisted Bill and Dick on their shoulders, bearing them through the surging, roaring mass of humanity that poured from the stands. They fought their way up the gym steps and down to the showers. The jubilant guards held the portals tight closed, refusing admission to all.

THE MONOTONOUS pounding of the surf was the only sound which penetrated the beleaguered house on old Tom Larkin's island. A beam of moonlight came through the fanlight over the big front door. Sheldon's long shadow passed and repassed through this in his slow prowl. He halted beside one of the barricaded windows, listening, then began his watch again, gun loosely in hand, another pistol strapped to his waist. He worked his way around the ghostly pieces of furniture, shrouded in white, which were piled against the door.

"Jim," he called softly down the hall.

"What is it, Dad?"

"Hear anything more?"

"They're still out there. I can hear them talking, arguing about something, but there's no sign of another attack. I can't understand why they don't rush us. There's enough of them!"

"Is Karlak with them?"

"I don't know. But the longer they delay, Dad,

the better for us. Those boys must have sent word to Tom by this time. He'll come with Bob."

Silence.

Then Sheldon called, "Any sound from the boy?"

"No. I put something for him to eat in the room but I didn't see him and he didn't speak."

"That's the safest place for him, in there. If that gang breaks in we'll have to go down into the passage ourselves. Watch out, Jim. That terrific crashing this afternoon means something, be sure of that."

Floorboards creaked as Sheldon went back to his post.

RUSHING through the darkness cars, summoned by the clicking telegraph, were racing toward the lonely village of Black Hill, Maine. There'd be no slip-up this time. The chair wouldn't be cheated of Stewart Sheldon. But the machine driven by Tom Larkin and followed by the police car was far in the lead. It swept down the long slope into Black Hill, turned into Main Street and stopped, to get information. From the glare of light far down the street came sounds of wild, triumphant cheering and the blasting of a band. The police siren shrieked through the happy blare of sound as the cars got under way.

Down in the mad hilarity and elation of the Black Hill team's dressing room Dick and Bill who were struggling to escape their well wishers and finish dressing, heard it and stared at each other. With one leap they made for the door, shouting "Good-byes" and "Good lucks" to all the applauding team.

Little Happy Landings, who had been trying to get to Bill all night, seized him now as he was tearing past. "Will you ottograft this scoah cahd fo' me, Mistah Bill?"

"Sure," Bill grabbed it. "Come around to Miss Adams' for it tomorrow morning!" he flung over his shoulder, as he and Dick crashed through a knot of rabid fans who wanted to carry him. They reached Larkin's car just as it was pulling out for Miss Adams', and leaped aboard.

CHAPTER XII

Down in the chill darkness of the secret passage Smiley shifted his cramped position wearily, listening. For a moment he imagined he caught a sound from above ground; from beyond the mass of earth and fallen timbers which held him and his pursuer trapped. The luminous figures on the dial of his wrist watch, appearing green and disembodied in the utter blackness, pointed to nearly one o'clock, which meant that he had been entombed here in this L-shaped length of tunnel almost twelve hours—since early afternoon.

He bent his icy fingers in upon his palms to warm them.

Why didn't help come? Sheldon and Jim couldn't, he knew, but why didn't Dick and Bill come? They must have sent Jim's message to Larkin for help hours ago. They should have reached the island by now.

Stealthily Smiley turned his head toward the lower part of the tunnel. His eyes were wide open but he could catch no glimmer in the darkness. After a